Special thanks to all the people that have supported this book and have supported me throughout the years of writing. I hope you enjoy this as much as I enjoyed the last 4 years bringing this story to life.

This Book is dedicated to a dear friend and Editor Sarah Morrish,

without her this story wouldn't be published.

Music. A gentle, familiar tune echoed through the narrow hallways as

Liv strode with haste through the corridors of the house. She could not

figure out where the music was coming from.

Her curiosity piqued, finding herself following the melody down the hall;

the translucent blue dress danced around her legs, chasing the beautiful

song, it continued to get louder, as if it was teasing her to find the source.

The music seemed to be coming from her left, so she turned towards a

tight passageway, only to be greeted with a dead end. Her dress floated

down to the knee as she paused briefly. Thinking to herself, something

seemed off. Like it shouldn't have existed. The walls around her were

cold to the touch and the light seemed to avoid reaching them. Yet the music was clear as day. However, something was peculiar. Liv rested her

forehead against the wall and exhaled. As she sighed, she felt a cool

breeze and stumbled forward slightly. To her astonishment the wall

slowly started to move. She stepped back as the wall revealed a dark

room, where the source of the music was. There. She had found… The

boy within the walls.

Chapter One

They say the first day is always the hardest. But, for Olivia, it would be

the day that forever changed her life. Olivia Osmund. Her parents were

proud as ever as she had just successfully transferred in at the Aumont

Academy. A high elite university that only the rich could go to. For

Olivia - a petite, blonde, skinny, and rather shy girl- had somehow;

managed to work hard enough to transfer within the echelons of the

university. Coming from no money herself it was a big deal too.

Considering her parents wouldn't let her on the joyride of money they

were hoarding away.

"We are so proud of you honey; you'll do great there," Olivia's mother

snivelled as she wiped a dishonest tear away from her eye.

Even though Olivia sensed a fake sort of comfort, her parents were still

keeping up the emotional pretence about letting their baby girl fly from

the nest.

"Don't worry mum. As soon as I settle in, I will get a housewarming

organised," Olivia smiled assuredly

"You'll do just fine Liv," Her father added, clearing his throat bruskly.

He was the one who suggested that Aumont Academy was the place,

since she couldn't stay at her old university any longer, due to Liv's

parents wanting to live on a fancy cruise ship, with all-inclusive

champagne. Her father lifted the last

of the medium sized brown boxes and placed it at the foot of the brand-new doorway.

"That's everything, it's best that we let you get settled in now," her father huffed as he stepped out of the doorway.

Her mother stood by the car sobbing silently unable to speak as if she was losing her only child. Walking towards her mother, she embraced her tightly. Though she gauged the pity was more than likely to be self-serving, she walked towards her mother and embrace her tightly.

"Don't worry, I'll come and visit as much as I can, you're also welcome anytime mum. I love you," Liv consoled.

One last time, her parents gave a tight squeeze. Before getting into the car and driving off, leaving Liv alone in the new home.

"Looks like I should get a cat," she quipped, laughing under her breath.

Picking up the boxes that her father left in the doorway, she placed them down a little further in the hall and closed the door behind her, beginning the process of unpacking.

Liv had never lived on her own and being in a house that was as silent as the grave was unsettling. Her house was empty, except for a circular medium dining table, a two seated, almost pristine, sofa and a bed that seemed untarnished to be left behind. Perhaps the previous owners had forgotten it? Nevertheless, Liv was grateful that the previous owners had left the basics.

It was more than her parents would ever do… Lifting a couple more boxes into the kitchen, she placed the remaining one onto the dining

8

table. Liv opened the box and on the very top of the pile of CDs and records she decided to bring, was a family photo. She frowned at it as it looked so superficial. In the photo Liv was standing awkwardly in between her mother and father and both of them were smiling as if they had just won the lottery.

She hated photos of herself, but she loathed the way her mother and father looked like they actually cared. It was all a carefully orchestrated façade, keeping up appearances, making sure no feathers were ruffled. After letting a long sigh, the photo was placed down next to the sink in the kitchen. She couldn't help but wonder to herself whether her father had chosen Aumont Academy because it was furthest away from home? Were they trying to be rid of their daughter? Liv couldn't stay at her previous university because her parents were planning on going on

9

expensive cruises alone together and Liv wouldn't be able to cope in that

house. Shaking her head trying to move on from the family issues;

bending down to pick up the box of records and CDs to her room. Liv

was stunned at how well furnished her room was, it was like she didn't

have to take a trip to IKEA after all.

After a couple of hours unpacking Liv finally felt like she was at home.

All the CDs that were brought, were stacked nicely on the new desk, and

her record player was also placed on the bedside table. The reason why

she had a record player on the bedside table instead of a lamp was that

she loved music and would rather wake up to the sound of it than the

pigeons cooing in the rising of the sun and the wind meandering between

the branches of the trees. Her room was finally decorated with the art she

created and artists that inspired her all over the walls, - giving the room more colour rather than the minimalistic look. Her books for tomorrow were neatly stacked on the desk too, books for her myths and legends lecture as well as several history books from the ancient history of Egypt to Nazi Germany and the World Wars. Liv looked at her phone and realised she had no calls or texts from her mother or father.

"Looks like they've already forgotten about me," Liv sighed, a little despondent but not entirely surprised.

She wasn't one of those girls that was extremely upset because her parents didn't really care for her well -being, or extremely relieved that they had left her alone. In fact, Liv seemed unusually okay with it. She understood that her parents didn't give her any of their money, she knew to get to where they were, she had to work for it. However, they acted so distant, it was like they were never really her parents in the first place.

Liv glanced out the window and realised it was getting late; watching as the sun went down, painting the sky with beautiful shades of pinks and oranges. Liv always admired the beauty of nature and how it was able to create such art by doing nothing- simply existing.

Just then, with a shock of realisation, she had been so busy unpacking she had forgot to go shopping for food, which the house was lacking. Luckily, Liv remembered that there was a grocery store that they passed, whilst being driven to the new home.

Rushing to the kitchen to grab the keys off the kitchen side; hoping she could make it in time before the store closed. The store was within walking distance, which was ideal because it meant she didn't have to try find someone to take her. Approaching the store, it seemed quiet; there was barely any cars in the carpark although, one car caught Liv's eye. It was a black BMW 6 series, meaning whoever owned that car was clearly either rich or famous. Turning her head away from the car and focusing her attention on getting food, then going home for a good night's sleep, before the big day tomorrow.

Liv grasped hold of a trolley and wheeled it into the store; throwing in a few vegetable bags and a bag of apples, as well as a week's worth of ready meals and stocked up on enough chocolate to feed an army. Judging herself on how much chocolate she was going to buy, she shrugged and made her way to the checkout. There, in front of her, were four people who were very well dressed considering it was only a grocery shop they were going to. There was a tall, beautiful woman with

13

a pointed chin, who seemed no older than her mid 40's. She had jet-

black hair which was scraped back into a tight perfect bun which gave

Liv head teacher vibes. Next to her was a man similar in age to the

woman, he was wearing a white coat which gave Liv the impression that

he was a doctor and must have just finished his shift. He was slightly

shorter than the woman next to him. However, his stature was built, and

he had reddish brown hair that was sleeked back. Behind the couple were

two younger adults, one a female who looked a couple years younger

than Liv; like the older man, she also had reddish brown hair that

cascaded down her lower back and she was pinching and prodding the

boy who was stood behind them. He must have been slightly older than

Liv, he had his arms crossed and seemed agitated with the girl. Assuming

that must have been his younger sister-, by the way she was teasing him.

14

The boy was similar to the older woman in height, he too-, had raven

black hair, which was slightly tousled like he had been running his

fingers through it too much. Realising she was staring too long; Liv kept

her head down and proceeded to the checkout. After loading her

shopping on the belt, she skilfully managed to pack all her shopping into

two bags. Walking out of the store; the four adults from before were

loading their car. She glanced over and realised they were the ones who

owned the 6 Series. As three of them got into the car the youngest female

was staring back directly at Liv. She froze, embarrassed she was caught

staring at the car again. The youngest female just smiled at her softly and

waved. Surprised, shocked and a little confused Liv waved back. That

was strange, she didn't know the girl so why did she wave?

Liv shrugged the weird encounter off and made her way back to the

house; her grocery bags was still intact, and successfully got back to her

house in one piece with all the groceries.

By the time Liv had got back it had started getting dark. She unlocked

the door and dumped her groceries on the side; closing the door behind,

hearing a faint buzz in the kitchen, she got a text from her mother.

Picture Attachment: We Miss You!

The picture was of her mother and father holding a glass of champagne

each. Typical. It hadn't even been 12 hours and they were already

celebrating of getting rid of her. Rolling her eyes at the picture and just

texted back:

Miss You Guys' too x.

If Liv was given an option to either live on a desert island alone or with

her parents, she'd probably choose the island.

She put her groceries away and chucked in a ready meal in the

microwave. Cooking was never her best talent, so it was the simplest

thing she could whip up, without giving herself food poisoning. Whilst

she ate, she looked at her phone *22:30PM*. It was getting pretty late so

Liv decided to clean her plate and call it a night, hoping now would be

enough sleep before her new adventure at Aumont Academy.

Chapter Two

Rudely awakened by the alarm trilling through the phone, a groan was

heard from beneath the duvet. Switching off the monotonous blare, Liv

arose from the bed, walking towards her records, she picked up the

record called Dark side of the moon, and placed it on the record player;

the song 'Money' started to play as she went for a shower. This was her

first time entering the bathroom surprisingly, shrugging the pyjamas that

clung to her body off, as she stepped into the shower. The water was

fresh and stung her eyes a little-, - clearly a good night sleep was

achieved, the music from her room ricocheted around the bathroom as

18

Liv finished showering. Hugging a towel, she re-entered the bedroom to

pick out the best outfit for the first day.

Picked straight out of the wardrobe was a pastel pink off the shoulder top

which flared at the sleeve and a pair of white jeans that she decided to

finish off with a pair of pale blue Converses. Grabbing some breakfast,

quickly before leaving, she took one final glance at what she was

wearing and left the house. The Academy was a few miles away. Without

a car, Liv would have to catch the bus until she saved up for one. It

wasn't that she couldn't drive, it was just her old campus was within

feasible walking distance, so she had no need for one. However, she felt

a wave of regret on not getting one as she had to catch the bus.

 Being shy had its downfalls, as it meant Liv became incredibly anxious

on public transport, with people staring as if there was a new shiny phone that had just been released. Shaking her head, she attempted to

ignore the intrusive thought that plagued her mind. It couldn't be that

bad? After all, it was only a short bus ride.

 The bus stop was next to the store, and luckily no one had arrived yet.

Liv stood patiently at the stop, remembering how weird that family was,

with their expensive car and that girl. How she randomly waved at her,

Liv really had to stop daydreaming or reminiscing on past events.

It was only going to cause trouble for her. A few moments later the bus

arrived, hopping on to the bus and with a sigh of relief, there were only a

few others that caught the bus. Filing her way to the back slowly, the

others on the bus were all in their own world, which Liv was grateful for.

It didn't matter - they perceived her as much as she perceived them, and

this comforted her.

20

This seemed like a great start to a first day, no awkward bus drive and

Liv actually felt pretty confident on how she looked like which was a

first.

After half an hour, the bus arrived at Aumont Academy. The Academy

looked like it was built around the 19th Century, it wasn't as big as Liv

thought it would be, the entrance was magnificent, the steps were made

from marble, and around the doors were stone figures in archways, like

the La Sagrada Familia in Barcelona. The figures seemed familiar, but

Liv couldn't put her finger on why. Behind the Academy was a long

driveway that led to a pair of large gothic iron gates. From a distance Liv

could make out a large building almost looking like a majestic manor of

sort. Stepping through the entrance of the Academy, to her astonishment,

she was shocked on how modern it was inside compared to the outside.

21

"Looks can be deceiving are they not?" A voice spoke, causing Liv to

jump.

To her side was a woman greying from age, she was holding a large

folder and a couple of books on top.

"I am Penny, I work as the receptionist and register new students who are

joining us. I don't recall seeing your face here before. Welcome to

Aumont Academy, follow me." Penny explained cheerfully.

Liv followed Penny through a set of double doors to a desk which was

placed in the centre of the room. Penny dumped her folders and books on

the desk next to a Mac computer. She plopped down into the leather seat

that was behind the desk and slid a pair of large red frames on her face.

Liv thought Penny was sweet in a grandmother kind of way. Suppose she kind of was to the Academy as she was the one looking after the

students' files and such.

"What's your name my dear?" Penny asked.

"Olivia Osmund, I am transferring." Liv replied suddenly, as if she was

put on the spot.

Penny giggled to herself noticing how jumpy Liv sounded.

"Just a second dear, I'll see if I can find you." Penny smiled; her fingers

tapped on the keyboard with lightning speed.

For an old woman she was pretty good with technology, Liv stood and

leant on the desk in front.

"Ah there we go, so the classes you are in are Myths and legends with

Ms. Aumont, and Classic History with Mr. Jones. I'll print off your

timetable and a map and let you get on. -" Penny expounded.

23

"Thank you so much, you've been a big help." Liv smiled politely.

Penny handed her timetable and a map to her and waved her off. Ms.

Aumont? Liv felt a little nervous as that must be one of the Aumont's

that founded this academy. She was surprised that there wasn't a student

rep or guide to help her get familiar with where each lecture was.

Suppose it was part of the Academy's independence scheme that was

suggested on their website. It was also in the middle of semester, so that

didn't help when Liv already knew she had to catch up big time in the

lectures she was taking. Or at least, make some friends so she could copy

notes from them from the beginning of the semester. Liv looked at the

map and saw that her Myths and Legends class was upstairs on the

second floor, in room 216P. Her history class was in 109BD which was

on the first floor. Looking around, Liv could see that this Academy was

24

flooded with the rich and famous, they must've paid thousands to get a

place here. Liv kept her head down as she suddenly felt out of place as

everyone seemed to have been dressed in high end clothing. The kind

that had no prices on so if you had to ask for the price you clearly

couldn't afford it. Liv took a deep breath to stop herself from panicking

over her cheap off the shoulder top and jeans she was wearing. Surely,

they were all adults and wouldn't take notice of what she was wearing?

Walking through the corridors a couple of girls and two guys strolled by.

One of the guy's Liv recognised he was tall, dark haired… That was it!

The guy from the grocery store.

Too busy wondering where she had seen the guy from, she smacked right

into one of the girls walking from the opposite direction.

"Ugh! Watch where you are going freak." The girl in front of her

frowned pushing Liv back.

She was stick thin, mostly leg, and brunette, she had beady eyes and

wore too much makeup. Liv was shocked as she stumbled to the floor.

Ouch. The three others laughed as she fell.

"I'm sorry, but there was really no need to push me like that!" Liv

exclaimed, rubbing her head.

"You were in my way. Don't you even know who I am? Or are your

parents too poor to own a TV?" The Brunette questioned curtly.

What a bitch. Liv didn't even know who this girl was, and she was so

snotty like she was in high school still. Suppose that's what she gets for

going to a rich kid Academy.

The Brunette started waving in Liv's face and snapping her fingers.

26

"Erm, Hello? Aren't you even going to answer me freakoid?" She

goaded.

Liv, who was still on the floor, rolled her eyes and sighed in frustration.

"No, I don't know who you are. And I couldn't care less, now let me get

up." Liv replied back confrontationally.

As she started to get up, the Brunette waved at the other girl to come

forward. This one was slightly proportioned right and was red haired. As

Liv got to her knees the red head pushed her back down. Liv looked at

the boy from the grocery store who was looking away. The girls and the

guy walked off. Feeling ashamed that Liv had already gained an enemy,

she got to her feet. As she got up, a hand extended to her.

"Sorry about Catharine, she is a bitch most of the time to everyone, don't

take it personally." The boy from the grocery store said apologetically.

27

Liv slapped his hand away, got up and dusted herself off.

"I don't want your help. You should have stood up to her if you were that

concerned for me." Liv asserted.

The boy looked pained at Liv's sharp words as she pushed past him

focusing on getting to her History class. She rushed up the stairs and

entered the room 109DB.

Chapter Three

Still angered, Liv walked up the seminar room and sat down in the third aisle in the first chair she saw. She fumbled trying to get her books out and her notepad out and exhaled. To make matters worse, the guy from the grocery store came in with the other guy who was with Catherine and the red-headed girl. Liv kept her head down and sunk into her seat praying that they didn't notice her. Unfortunately, her fears came to fruition, and they did notice her, the other guy who was with grocery guy approached her.

"Hey Sweetie, don't you look all cute with your erm… history books?"

The guy flirted, confused why Liv had history books.

29

Both the guys wore blue jerseys and the one who spoke to her was

holding a basketball and the grocery guy just stood beside him

flawlessly.

"Well yeah, I did its part of the course? And don't call me sweetie." Liv

bluntly questioned.

Both of the guys sniggered at her and walked to the next row and sat

behind her. Great, just what she needed. As the time on her phone turned

to *10AM*, the room flooded with other students who made their way to

their seats. Suddenly, a wave of regret swept over Liv, as other students

started looking at her history books funnily. Before she could make a get-

away. A middle- aged man with slicked back jet black hair walked in, Liv

thought she had seen him somewhere before. Was it the man from the grocery store? The lecturers' appearance was uncanny to the other mans

from before, however, Liv couldn't be too sure if it was.

"Settle down everyone, has everyone read their Shakespeare sonnet?"

The lecturer questioned.

Shakespeare sonnet? That can't be right... If that was the case then- oh

no... Liv fumbled around looking for her timetable. 109BD, she had

gotten the rooms mixed up.

Liv froze, trying not to freak out that she was in the wrong class, she

thought it was best to sit and wait until the lecturer stopped talking. For

the mean time she picked up her pen and started writing notes to make it

look like she was doing something. She hated English Literature with a

passion. What was the point trying to describe what something _could_

mean, when the meaning is as clear as day? Trying to concentrate on

31

what the lecturer was saying became extremely difficult, as the guys at

the back were texting and their phones would go off every 5 seconds as

well as laughing and talking to each other. Liv started getting aggravated

with them as she was really trying to understand what was going on. But

she couldn't take the constant background noise going on behind her.

"Will you stop disrupting I'm trying to understand what's going on!" Liv

hissed at the guys behind her.

Grocery boy just smiled and leaned forward over his desk,

"If you weren't so rude earlier, I would have shown you the way to your

history lecture myself." He teased.

"I was the rude one well you and your bitch of a friend started I-"

"Am I interrupting something Mr. Aumont? If not, can we get back to

topic please." The lecturer scolded.

Infuriated by the comment Liv didn't take notice what the grocery guy

was called.

"Sh, now you're going to get us both into a load of trouble in a minute."

Grocery boy teased giving Liv a playful wink.

"You're the one who didn't have a decency to switch your stupid phone

on silent, plus, you were giggling like a pair of little girls back there."

Liv hissed again.

The other guy was nudging the grocery boy, to stop leaning over as the

lecturer was glaring at both him and Liv.

"That's it. Congratulations! You two have become project partners and

will spend at least two hours of group work on comparing sonnet 18 and

the balcony scene from Romeo and Juliet. You will present what you

found out to the whole of the class. Oh, and one more thing, Eric, move

33

next to the lovely lady in front of you. I'll speak to you both at the end."

The lecturer motioned angrily, his green eyes flashing with frustration.

Eric looked over at the other guy sat next to him, got up from his seat

and dropped into the seat next to Liv, propping his feet up on his desk.

"Good going. Asshole." Liv whispered under her breath, just at enough

volume that only Eric could hear it.

Eric rolled his beautiful brown eyes and ran his fingers through his

messy black hair. Finally, after being scolded and being paired with one

of the cutest yet irritatingly infuriating guys Liv has known, she could

finally focus on taking notes. After the lecture was over Liv started

getting a headache and packed her things away. Rubbing her forehead,

she made her way towards the door.

"Where do you think you're going miss?" the lecturer asked.

34

"This has all just been a big misunderstanding, I was supposed to head to

109BD but ended up here, I am supposed to be taking history." Liv

explained.

"Right. I see you must be the new girl that was transferring. What's your

name?" The lecturer asked again.

"Olivia, Liv Osmond." She replied.

Eric was still sat with his feet up on the desk and his eyes were fixated

on Olivia, like he was in a trance. This bugged her and she avoided

looking his way.

"Then it's settled, I will inform Penny to change your timetable to

Literature with me, considering you just wandered in here and disturbed

the lecture on your first day." The lecturer said cheerfully as he walked

out of the room.

35

"Bu-" Liv started then sighed.

If first days couldn't get any crappier. Eric finally decided to get up from the seat and make his way down. He walked past Liv and stood in the doorway.

"So, Liv, when do you want to get started on this project? Ajax doesn't really bluff on these kinds of things." Eric asked.

"I don't know soon I guess." She sighed.

Eric frowned; he knew that Liv didn't like him much, he was only trying to help the situation as he caused it. He turned to her and smiled devilishly.

"Then it's settled. I'll come to yours tomorrow after lecture and I'll decipher Romeo and Juliet's balcony scene whilst you decode sonnet 18?" He suggested.

36

Liv was too tired to continue fighting with Eric, so she just nodded in agreement, even though she wasn't happy about him inviting himself over to her place. He smiled softly trying to reassure Liv, however his attempt didn't succeed. He sidled past her and made his way to his next lecture.

Liv took the long way to Myths and Legends as she didn't really want to cross war paths with Catherine again.

Walking upstairs, she walked past the music rooms. As she paced past them, something drew her back.

 The sweet soothing sound of a piano could be heard through the walls of one of the rooms, Liv slowed her pace so she could listen a little longer. Each note travelled through her body as she absorbed the music in. Then the tune slightly changed, it was a song that sounded so familiar to her, but she knew she'd never heard of it before. Realising the time, Liv saw

that it was almost time for her next lecture. Coming out of the musical

trance she was in she picked up the pace towards room 216P. Luckily,

Liv had made it in time. This room wasn't like her other room where

there were rows climbing up all the way to the back of the room. This

room was a lot smaller, and the desks were in a U shape around a fancy

projector board.

Liv sat down at the end desk of the U shape, and as before, got all the

books and the notepad out.

A few moments passed, as 6 more students entered the room. Only six?

This course clearly wasn't very popular with people, though Liv was

grateful, the less people the less drama that would happen in there. After

all the students made it, in followed a tall slim woman, her charcoal hair

38

was scraped back into a tight bun. Like the English lecturer, her eyes

were a piercing green, they both looked oddly similar to one another Liv

thought to herself. The woman that was from before as well, she must me

the famous Ms. Aumont, Penny was on about. She was wearing an

extremely elegant power suit, which made her looked like she had

walked off the red carpet promoting the strong female type.

"Now then, let's cut to it." Ms. Aumont sharply spoke.

Her voice was chilling, if not a little intimidating, Liv was just glad that

Eric wasn't in this class to get her in trouble.

"We will begin looking at the Norse Gods and The Aesir. Can anyone tell

me what the Aesir are?" Ms. Aumont quizzed the class.

Liv stuck her hand up as if she was back in school, Ms. Aumont looked

at her and nodded, indicating Liv to speak.

"The Aesir were the main gods of the pantheon, most of the Gods that were in the Aesir were Odin and his wife Frigg and Thor the son of Odin." Liv explained quickly.

Expecting a look of delight that she had got the answer right, Ms. Aumont frowned at her. Liv was confused by the reaction as she didn't know what she did wrong.

"Correct, and can anyone tell me what Ragnarök is?" She asked again bluntly.

"It is the Norse version of doomsday." Liv answered again.

"Thank you, Miss. Osmund. However, next time you feel your itch to know everything please refrain of talking when you were not spoken to directly." Ms. Aumont scolded coldly.

"I just answered your-"

"For once can you just let someone else answer the questions, Olivia? No one likes a know it all." Ms. Aumont cut off slyly.

For the rest of the time being Olivia sat there in silence and kept her head down scribbling notes on the Norse god profiles such as Odin, Figg, Thor, Loki, and Hel. As the lecture finally finished up Liv was the first one out and she couldn't wait to get home and forget about today.

Walking out of the Academy out of the student car park she could hear Eric's voice calling her. She pretended that she couldn't hear it until he caught up with her.

"Hey. Olivia? Didn't you hear me shouting for you?" Eric asked.

His brown eyes turned an amber, honey like colour as the sun caught them.

"Oh no, I was too busy trying to get home." Liv said bluntly.

41

"Look I know you probably had a shitty first day but trust me first days are always bad here." Eric attempted to reassure her.

Liv still didn't like him; however, his words did bring her some comfort and it was nice to know it wasn't just her first day that had sucked here.

"Thanks, but I really need to be going." Liv replied quickly.

Trying to make a quick escape, Eric grabbed her hand and scribbled something on it.

"Hey what are you doing!" Liv exclaimed.

"Relax its only my phone number, you're going to need it, especially now that we are partners." Eric teased, giving her hand a kiss as he walked away before Liv could protest anymore. However, as he walked away, she could see in the distance... Catherine. The look of horror

42

mixed with jealousy was written all over it. Liv quickly looked away and

made her way to the bus stop. Yep, she had just been given a death

sentence for tomorrow. And how dare Eric kiss her hand? The cockiness

of a rich kid really did get under Liv's skin…!

*

*

As Liv got home, she kicked off her blue converse and made a bee line

for her room. She didn't feel like making any food or eating in general,

to be frank, she thought the best thing she could do was go straight to

bed after the most disastrous day she'd had.

As she was getting ready for bed, she glanced at her hand and realised

she'd better save Eric's number, as much as she would hate to admit it,

he was right she was going to need it if they were expected to work

together.

She decided to punch his number in and shoot him a text:

It's Liv BTW, Not Olivia.

As she hit sent, she walked towards the bed and laid down. After a

couple of moments her phone vibrated:

Right Liv. Gotcha. C U tomorrow.

Chapter Four

Waking up the next day, Liv felt awful. As her vision came too, Liv

realised that she had slept in her clothes instead of getting ready for bed.

She reached for her phone which had happened to fall on the floor during

the night. Looking at the time her eyes widened: *9:30AM.* Crap! She was

going to be late for uni. She leaped out of her bed and made a bee line

for the bathroom. Rushing around, she washed her face and brushed her

teeth rapidly, pealing out of her outfit from yesterday, and chucking on a

pair of jeans and a hoodie from her wardrobe.

Smoothing the out of place hairs on her head, she swiftly wacked her

hair up in an untidy bun and darted out of the house.

Sprinting down towards the bus stop, Liv could see that the bus was

already there. Running as fast as her legs would take her, she bolted

towards the bus. Just as Liv arrived, the bus had closed its doors but then,

after a second or two, reopened them.

"You're lucky I didn't just drive off then Miss." The driver cautioned.

"Thank you for not." Liv panted as she made her way to the back of the

bus.

This time, people were staring at her, as she walked towards the back

people started shuffling to the outward seats so she wouldn't sit next to

them. Catching her reflection Liv could see why.

Her face was as red as a tomato, her hair was a complete mess. In fact,

she might as well have been a tomato with the way her hair was sticking

out all over the place. Embarrassed with herself, she sat down and shied

47

away from everyone. Coming to her senses, Liv tried to smooth her hair

down on the way to the campus. Looking down, Liv realised that she was

dressed as if she were homeless: great, another reason why people were

probably staring at her.

Approaching the campus, Liv allowed everyone to get off the bus before

she did, the redness in her cheeks had died down and her wreck of a hair

started to calm. She checked the time on her phone; *9:55AM*. Wasting no

time, she walked inside and approached Penny, who was sitting at her

desk like she was yesterday.

"Ah Olivia, Mr. Adler has requested that you are in his lecture now, I

have informed Mr. Jones and your new timetable has been approved."

Penny explained as she handed Liv her schedule.

48

Liv sighed, accepting defeat as she grabbed the new timetable and stared

blankly at it. This was all Eric's fault. If he didn't disturb her, she

wouldn't have got into this mess in the first place, Liv thought to herself.

Giving her hair one last smooth down she made her way back through

the corridors towards the dreaded 109DB. Avoiding the way she went

yesterday, Liv decided to take a different route to her new class.

Falling into a jog, Liv managed to step through the door dead on

9:59AM. Looking up towards her seat, there he was. Feet up on the seat

in front, his dark hair was a mess like he had also been rushing, which

had made Liv feel a little more comfortable with her badly smoothed

down hair as Eric's hair was almost identical to hers. Smiling to herself

bemusedly over it, she walked up to her seat. Perhaps he wasn't an ass after all. Eric gave Liv a flashy smile and stretched his arm over her chair.

"Sup partner." He teased.

Instantly took back the thought he wasn't an ass.

"Don't call me that. Have you taken any notes on any of the sonnets or Romeo & Juliet?" Liv asked sharply.

"Nope. Who needs notes on books when there are films?" Eric laughed.

Liv glared coldly at Eric before trying to calm the back of her mind from panicking.

Eric's smile turned from a teasing one to a softer one.

"Relax, here take this, we can go through these notes through this double period. Don't worry I'll dumb it down for you." Eric reassured.

Pulling out from a rucksack behind him Eric handed a notepad filled

with labels sticking out and stacked with piles of notes.

Quickly flicking through the notes Liv sighed with relief.

"Wow, so from sports pro to nerd?" Liv teased.

Eric furrowed his brow.

"No, I'm not into sports and I actually stole these from my uncle, he

loves Shakespeare." Eric shot back at her.

Liv didn't know how to reply to that, so she decided not to respond.

Checking her phone, it read *10:00AM*, the last of the class were settling

and Eric had moved his feet off the back of the seat in front, however, he

still rested his arm on the back of Liv's seat. From across the room, she

could see one of Catherine's minions glancing over and texting. Liv fidgeted in her seat uncomfortably, as Mr. Adler walked in and addressed

the class Liv nudged Eric.

"I don't mean to be rude, but could you move your arm off my seat

please?" Liv whispered trying not to get in trouble again.

Looking across the class Eric could see Catherine's minion and his other

friend laughing and texting. Liv sank into her chair feeling uneasy being

watched.

Eric nudged her back.

"Hey, don't worry, I'll deal with those idiots." Eric whispered, gesturing

to the couple across the room.

"Aren't they your friends though?" Liv asked.

"Just because I hang around them, doesn't make them my friends." Eric

replied.

Ignoring the minions doing their bidding, Liv and Eric both went through

the notes Eric had stolen off his uncle.

"So, the Capulets and the Montagues are rivalling families however,

Romeo and Juliet fell in love and eloped despite of the family's

disapproval." Eric began to explain.

Liv studied all the brightly highlighted notes.

"Right, so its boy meets girl, family dispute, fake deaths becoming real

deaths?" Liv summarised waiting for approval.

Eric smiled and nodded, running his fingers through his hair once more

before flicking the next page of his copy of the play.

"You know, you're actually not that bad." Liv smiled.

"And you seem not to have a stick somewhere up there." Eric laughed

pointing towards Liv's backside.

Liv gave him a playful shove as they continued decoding the play.

"Looks like pairing you both together has brought the best out of the pair

of you." Mr. Adler smiled as he walked up and looked over the notes.

"Yeah, we've made progress, Romeo and Juliet is almost making sense

just have to do the sonnet." Liv replied.

Mr. Adler looked over at the notes laughed and turn back walking down

back to the front of the class.

"Oh Eric, make sure you return those notes." He added.

Looking astonished Liv looked at Eric.

"How'd he know you stole them?" she asked.

"No reason, come on its lunch time you deserve a break." Eric quickly

answered back.

Packing up their things, Liv and Eric both left the lecture room.

54

"See you tomorrow, I'll text you any information that I forgot."

"Right yeah have fun with your not so- called friends." Liv replied.

Eric laughed softly shaking his head as he parted ways with Liv.

Feeling hungry Liv, quickly checked the time on her phone *1:30PM.* She

had not been to the canteen yet, so decided to go grab something to eat

there.

Making her way to the canteen Catherine's minions walked past her. The

red-haired girl who had previously pushed Liv barged into her.

"Watch where you're going freak! Oh- and just you wait till Catherine

finds you." The red-haired girl laughed spitefully wiggling her phone at

Liv.

"Oh Char, you didn't. Did you?" the guy who was previously sat next to

Eric teased swinging his arm around her shoulders.

55

Without replying they both walked off laughing in the distance.

Yet again, Liv felt like she was a piece of gum on someone's shoe. She looked down and continued her way to the canteen.

Approaching the canteen, the place boomed with chattering young adults to slightly older ones. Unlike any school, people weren't sat in cliques, everyone had just blended in which Liv admired and felt like she would settle in quite nicely. She queued in line to get her food which were served on white porcelain plates, the food wasn't bad either. There was a selection of pasta dishes to light lunches such as sandwiches and crisps. Liv grabbed one of the sandwiches and made her way towards a small circular table that was empty. Whilst enjoying her meal she could see a girl coming her way. Perhaps it was a potential new friend? As she approached closer Liv could see that the girl was marching over, not

56

looking happy. Before she realised who it was, she finished her lunch

and got up intending to avoid her. Catherine.

She had marched right up to Liv and blocked her from avoiding

confrontation. Behind Catherine were her two minions, Char and the boy

who hung out with Eric. Hoping Eric was there, Liv's heart sank as she

knew he wasn't able to save her this time. Closing any space between

Liv and herself, Catherine frowned.

"So, two little birds have told me you've been flirting with my

boyfriend?" She sneered.

Liv was shocked, she assumed that Catherine had referred to Eric.

"I- I haven't been flirting with him?" Liv stammered.

Pushing her to the table Catherine grabbed hold of her throat.

"Let's make one thing clear freak. Eric is mine so back the fuck off." She

hissed.

Behind her eyes Liv could see that she had the intent to do her harm

trying to grab her wrist and pull it away from her neck Catherine had

swung her fist into Liv's nose. A cracking noise came from Liv's face as

blood poured from her nose. As her fist made contact, Liv tried to use

her legs to shift Catherine off her. With that, Catherine gave her a punch

in the stomach. Everyone around were staring and no one was there to

help her, Catherine leaned in.

"Now do you understand what back off means now freak?" Catherine

whispered into Liv's ear.

"Y-y-yes." Liv stammered again.

She had started to feel dizzy, and her sight began to fuzz. Before

Catherine gave one final blow as a message to stay away, a hand grabbed

her tightly around her wrist. Liv couldn't make out who it was who

stopped Catherine, but she knew it was definitely a male.

"Enough." The voice snapped, his tone was low and sounded dangerous.

"I was just teaching her-"

"I don't care. Leave her alone, we are done here." He cut Catherine off.

Catherine got off Liv and retreated back to her place. The male figure

kneeled down to Liv handing her a tissue. Touching her nose her

fingertips came back stained red.

Her vision started to double, as she focused, she saw Eric in front of her,

his eyes filled with worry.

"Liv I'm so sorry…" Eric looked down.

59

As he apologised Liv felt her eyes sting as if someone had squeezed

lemon juice in them before she knew it hot tears started to stream down

her face.

"You said you would talk to them." Liv sobbed as she pushed past Eric

leaving him alone at the table.

Chapter Five

Bursting into the nearest bathroom, Liv sobbed. A mix of tears and blood tumbled down her face. Hiding herself in one of the stalls, she thought to herself how much she hated this uni. She had even started regretting leaving a home that didn't want her. Trying to pull herself together, Liv got up and stepped out of the stall, luckily no one was in there with her. She flicked the tap that was nearest to her and ran the cold water.

As it began to pool, Liv grabbed some tissue to sort out her bloody nose, washing the tears and blood away from her face. Looking back into the mirror wasn't Liv's usual reflection. In fact, the figure was wearing

61

scuffed up jeans which were ripped slightly, and her hoodie was a mess,

travelling up to her face

her eye was bloodshot and underneath it was starting to swell a darkish

purple.

Pulling her phone out of her pocket the display:

2 missed calls

Messages

Eric: Hey, look I'm sorry for what happened. Please let me explain.

Swiping to clear the notifications, she decided to go ask Penny for help

as she seemed to be the most useful person in this dump so far.

Heading towards the front desk, Liv put her hood up and kept her head

down trying not to draw attention to herself.

"Hey Penny, could you help me with something?" Liv whispered over

the desk.

Busy typing away Penny paused.

"Just one moment please." She sang.

Looking up from her monitor she shot up.

"Oh Miss Osmund! What happened?!" She exclaimed.

Gesturing her to shush, Penny understood and looked at her worryingly.

With that reaction Liv had thought that due to Penny's age the fright

would have given her a heart attack. But she had no one else to turn to.

"Could you help me clean this up please?" Liv asked quietly.

Penny nodded and came around to the same side where Liv was.

"Of course, dear, right this way." Penny replied.

Her tone again went from receptionist to concerned grandmother, even though they were not related. Guiding Liv into the office behind her desk, she sat Liv down and grabbed a cold compress and handed it to her.

"Here, this should help reduce the swelling, now let me guess, the person to give you that black eye wasn't Catherine Donal?" Penny asked raising an eyebrow which smoothed out some of her wrinkles on her forehead.

"How did you know?" Liv asked astonished at Penny's guess.

Penny sighed and looked at a small photo frame that was located on a filing cabinet.

"Unfortunately, that troubled girl, is my step granddaughter. She has always been a badun If you want to report this I completely understand." Penny empathised.

"It's fine, I doubt I will be here long enough to stay." Liv sighed with

despondence.

Penny put her hand on Liv's shoulder and squeezed it in a comforting

way.

"Just because today was a bad day, it doesn't mean you should give up.

You have so much potential in you Olivia, don't let anyone put you

down." Penny encouraged.

Liv smiled and placed her hand over Penny's.

"Thank you for everything Penny, I needed this." Liv sighed in relief.

"Anytime, I'll tell you what, take the rest of the day off, keep that cold

compress on and I'll inform your lecturers that you have gone home

sick." Penny advised.

Giving her one last squeeze Penny walked back to her chair and

continued with the typing she was previously doing before Liv disturbed

her.

Gathering her things and her cold compress Liv, made her way home and

decided to lie down for the remainder of the day.

*

*

After putting yesterday's disaster behind her, Liv examined her eye. The

bloodshot seemed to have died down, however, the purple shade was still

stamped under her eye. Luckily the swelling had gone down thanks to

Penny.

Looking around for a tube of foundation, Liv rummaged through some of

her stuff that she didn't unpack until she found a bottle. Trying to blend

out the purple, she managed to just disguise that she had a black eye.

On the bright side at least, she wasn't dressed as a hobo this time.

Getting her stuff together, Liv heard a car pull outside. Going to

investigate the vehicle, Liv looked out to see that Penny was outside her

house.

67

Stepping out the door with millions of questions Liv looked confused.

"Erm, Hello Penny what are you doing here?" Liv questioned.

"I still feel really awful about yesterday, I thought this is the least I can do to help you out and help save you a bit of money." Penny explained.

Appreciating the gesture Liv got in the car.

"Okay just this once I'll take you up on this offer, but please don't feel you need to turn up randomly at my house." Liv chuckled.

Penny smiled and drove off towards the Academy.

Surprisingly, it didn't take as long to drive there compared to the bus, in fact it cut the journey time in half. After being offered mint imperials most of the journey, Liv thanked Penny and made her way to her first lecture of the day, crossing her fingers that today would be a better day.

Making her way to Myth & Legends, Liv walked slowly past the music

department, and once again she could hear the soft plays of the piano.

Listening out, Liv could recognise that the song that was being played

was Moonlight Sonata in its 3rd movement. Walking past and allowing

the music fade naturally, Liv entered her lecture room. Ms. Aumont was

sat straight at her desk reading upon on the weekly news that was

happening in the area.

"Feeling better?" She asked putting the paper down and raising an

eyebrow.

Liv froze at the door, as she forgot that Penny had told Ms. Aumont that

she wouldn't be in.

"Er, yes thank you I-"

"Good then you best catch up on what you missed last lecture. We will be discussing the story of Idun today." Ms. Aumont cut off bluntly.

As Ms. Aumont got up and left, it gave Liv some time to catch up what she missed. Checking her phone, it read 8:45AM. As Liv accepted the lift from Penny, she got in earlier than usual, even though, she planned to come in early because. Liv was afraid that Ms. Aumont might skin her alive if she was late.

Catching up on what she missed last lecture, Liv started to research on Norse mythology. Googling in depth about Valhalla, the relationships between each god and how they originated.

After an hour of research, the other few students started coming in and sat down.

Ms. Aumont then reappeared, as soon as she stepped in the chattering of

students stopped.

"Right, let's get to it, today we will be looking at the story of Idun and

the legend of the golden apples." Ms. Aumont began to explain.

"So Idun, is an important key to the gods as if it wasn't for her guarding

the golden apples, they would lose their immortality." Ms. Aumont

continued.

Flicking through different slides Ms. Aumont handed out books that

where based on the legend of Idun and the golden apples.

"Now I am not a teacher, you will not be spoon fed by me, so you have

the rest of the lecture to continue to learn about the legend of the golden

apples and relationship between Hel and Idun." She bluntly put.

71

Doing more research Liv learned that Hel was Loki's daughter who was half alive and half dead and ruled the underworld. She also learned that Loki tried to kidnap Idun, which didn't last.

Sieving through all the information Liv stumbled upon "the sacrifice of Idun" reading through it, Idun was sacrificed to Hel as she desired her half dead side to be as beautiful and young as her alive side. To revive herself to a fully alive goddess Hel had to sacrifice Idun in order to retrieve on of her apples. Unfortunately, Hel wasn't successful and learned that sacrificing Idun would only get her to the mortal world, where Odin sent Hel to the underworld as punishment for killing another goddess.

Reading on the golden apples would not be given away unless the descendant of Idun gives consent to a descendant of Hel.

72

Stuck in her research Ms. Aumont towered over Liv.

"I have a job for you as you're the only student who has managed to research the entire legend of the golden apples, I'd like you to print this research for me and hand it in as an assignment." Ms. Aumont smirked.

Unsure if it was praise or mockery, Liv nodded and made a start on her new torture.

For the whole lecture, Ms. Aumont had set several different tasks for Liv and her alone while the rest of the class researched the myth the entire morning.

Walking to English was a breeze- no Catherine, Char or Eric which meant that it was looking like a good day for Liv after all.

As she walked past the music department, she saw Eric emerge from the door where the piano was usually playing. He was a few paces ahead and

Liv was glad, she didn't feel like talking to him as she was afraid it

would only get her into more trouble.

As she got to the English lecture room, she had caught up with Eric,

ignoring him while entering, Liv got to her seat and lead her stuff out

over the desk. Eric propped himself next to her and smiled.

"Hey! Mrs. Smiley." He joked, trying to lighten up the mood.

Liv ignored him and continued to study Sonnet 18 which made no sense

to her. Eric looked at her trying to figure out how he could get Liv to talk

to him.

Half an hour had passed, and Liv still was ignoring Eric. Eric had let a

long-exaggerated sigh and was leaning his face on his hand. Liv glance

quickly over and saw how fed up he was starting to look. He deserved it,

74

she thought to herself, if it wasn't for him, she wouldn't have gotten

punched in the face.

"How's the eye?" Eric sighed, pointing to his own eye.

His tone was sincere and seemed a little sad if not guilty.

"Sore. No thanks to your girlfriend." Liv replied bitterly.

She couldn't help it, she wanted to forgive him, but she was stubborn.

"She's not my… Never mind, you can't ignore me for the entire lecture,

after all we still have a project to do." Eric explained.

Liv again went silent; he did have a point if she ignored him, she

wouldn't get through this stupid class. Liv sighed in defeat.

"Fine you win, now help me with this Sonnet." Liv commanded.

Trying to fight off the twitch of a smile, Eric submitted and started to

explain how the sonnet had relevance to the play.

75

Chapter Six

"So, the main themes that links this scene to this sonnet is love, the difference between them is instead of exchanging compliments and showing their feelings, whereas Sonnet 18 is almost like a love letter."

Eric started to explain.

Liv listened and tried to understand what Eric was trying to explain.

"Eric, I don't think I understand any of this." Liv panicked.

Eric closed his stolen notes and smiled.

"It's okay, you've gone through a lot. I don't expect you to get your head around it first time." He grinned

He sounded like a teacher the way he tutored Liv, supporting her through

this project. It was nice for Liv as she didn't have to do all the work for a

change.

"Can I ask you something personal?" Liv asked.

Eric raised his eyebrow and ran his hand through his glossy black hair.

"Do I get a choice?" He asked back teasingly.

"No, I need to know to save my other eye! What's the deal with you and

Catherine?" Liv interrogated.

Whilst asking him the question she didn't know what lead her to asking,

but she could feel herself blushing for invading his personal life.

Eric rolled his eyes at the question,

"Nothing has ever happened between her and me, she has always had a thing for me, and it bugs her when she doesn't get what she wants. She's like a spoiled child." Eric laughed.

"Sooo… you are definitely single?" Liv wondered.

"Sounds like someone's eager." Eric teased.

The implication that Eric suggested made Liv go a bright scarlet colour.

"But yes. Have been for a while." Eric cleared his throat, trying to relieve the awkward embarrassment.

"You said yesterday you'd talk to them… Where were you when it all happened?" Liv asked again.

"I needed a place to escape, but don't worry they won't bother you ever again." Eric reassured.

"What do you mean a place to escape?" Liv asked.

79

"Ugh, are you really going to interrogate me all lecture?" Eric sighed in annoyance.

Liv looked down and continued with her work, realising that she had probably overstepped her boundaries with him.

"Sorry, I'm not used to lots of questions, girls tend to just swoon." Eric apologised.

However, the last remark seemed a bit big headed of him to say.

"Right ladies' man. Check. Doesn't like sports. Check. And likes to be the mysterious type. Check." Liv teased, pretending to write the list down.

Eric laughed at her doing so and shook his head.

"You really don't like me much. Do you?" He laughed softly.

"Not really, but you're growing on me." Liv smiled softly.

80

Disturbing their conversation, Mr. Adler addressed the lecture.

"Right, times up for today, I expect your projects to be in on Monday."

He informed the students.

"Right, so that's two days to get everything in a presentable shape. I

don't know what you reckon but we may need to work over this out of

uni hours." Liv explained trying not to sound too erratic or suggestive.

"How about your place?" Eric smiled.

Liv looked confused not feeling okay with his decision.

"You do owe me considering you weren't here, and we were supposed to

go to yours yesterday." He teased.

Frowning at him, Liv had almost forgotten how cocky he was the first

day.

"No. You need to stop inviting yourself over to my place. It's rude." Liv

snapped unintentionally, taking herself back with her own sharpness.

"Woah, it was only an idea." Eric responded holding his hands up in

surrender.

"Why is it that one minute you can be so sweet and the next you are a

complete ass?" Liv asked.

Something about him made her blood boil and she didn't know why.

"Liv… Chill it was only a suggestion." Eric spoke calmly.

Snapping back into the room Liv shook her head in confusion and looked

at Eric.

"I'm sorry, I think my head was hit too yesterday." Liv gasped.

She didn't know what came over her, it was like a rage had started up in

her for no reason. The rage was out of character for her, and she hadn't

82

ever got angry like that at anyone, it was almost like she wasn't in

control of her body.

"Look let's forget about it, if you're not okay with your place mine is

always an option." Eric grinned trying to realign the conversation and

glaze over any rumblings of confrontation. Liv was still confused trying

to figure out why she had flipped out, forgetting that she wasn't paying

attention to Eric.

Before she came back down to the ground, Eric was waving his hand in

front of her face.

"Hey, are you sure you're, okay? You don't look too good." Eric asked

worryingly.

"Yeah, I'm fine my place is good." Liv replied still half in the clouds.

83

"Look let's get something to eat and I'm taking you home." Eric advised.

Something wasn't right with Liv, but Eric couldn't think what it was he

had done wrong.

Putting his arm over Liv's shoulders, Eric supported her down the stairs

and towards the corridor.

"Look I'm fine I was lost in thought that was all." Liv reassured.

Walking through the corridor Liv and Eric both walked past Catherine

and her minions, Eric squeezed Liv's shoulder as they walked past,

however, Liv couldn't help but notice that Catherine was crying.

"What did you exactly say to her?" Liv asked.

"Huh? Nothing really, just to leave you alone." Eric replied quickly.

Liv became a little cautious of Eric because Catherine wasn't the type of

girl to cry over a little rejection. Shifting his arm off her shoulder she

84

walked next to him with a slight bit of distance between them. As they

continued walking a small brown- haired girl came bounding Eric's way.

As she homed in closer Liv could see that it was the girl who was

annoying Eric at the grocery store.

Smacking into Eric the girl put her fist into his stomach.

"Sup douchebag." She sang.

"Oof. Fi, you really didn't have to do that." Eric mumbled.

Liv giggled to herself as the brown-haired girl turned towards her.

"You're that girl from the grocery store I saw!" She shrieked in

excitement.

"See Eric! I told you I wasn't seeing things, she even waved back at me."

She continued.

Eric looked at her strangely and then looked at Liv for confirmation.

85

"Yeah, I saw you too. I was just admiring your car that you all got into."

Liv laughed nervously, forgetting that she was caught staring like a

creep.

"Ahh! I'm just so glad that you were real. My name is Ophelia, call me

Fi for short." Ophelia smiled.

"Nice to meet you Fi, I'm Olivia, Liv for short." Liv introduced.

Ophelia gasped and placed her hands over her mouth.

"Why would you shorten such a pretty name!" Ophelia gasped.

"Back at ya." Liv giggled.

"I love her! Eric you better keep this one!" Ophelia teased and winked at

him.

"She's just a friend Fi, now where we are going for lunch?" Eric asked.

"By the steps as always duh, really, how on earth did you get the stupid

gene." Ophelia laughed.

Rolling his eyes, Eric gave Ophelia a playful shove forward and turned

to Liv.

"Sister I'm guessing?" Liv asked smiling as she asked.

"Yeah, how'd you guess haha. Look I know you've had a hard time…

Why don't you have lunch with Fi and me, Fi could really use with a

female friend." Eric offered.

Skipping back Ophelia grabbed Liv's hand.

"She doesn't get a choice- I am now adopting her as my new BFF," She

declared.

Dragging Liv ahead, Ophelia lead her to the steps. For someone petite,

she was strong.

Pulling her down to sit, Liv sat next to Ophelia and Eric sat on a step

lower spreading himself over the step he was on. Both Ophelia and Eric

pulled out identical lunches.

"What ya make today for us then Eric." Ophelia asked.

"Shut up and eat it and you'll find out." Eric grinned

Liv smiled, how she wished that she wasn't the only child. Disturbing

her thoughts, Eric was nudging her leg.

"Here. Eat. I know that you don't pack lunch." Eric insisted.

Handing over half of his sandwich Liv, took it and bit into it.

"Thanks," She accepted, with her mouthful of sandwich.

"Mmm, my favourite, Peanut butter and banana." Ophelia chimed.

Liv looked at her sandwich, she hated peanut butter, so she double checked to make sure it wasn't. Luckily for her Eric had made himself a BLT.

"Liv, how long have you known my douche of a brother for?" Ophelia asked, stuffing more of her sandwich in her mouth.

"Well... Not long, we've only known each other a little while and thanks to him I'm now stuck in an English lecture with him." Liv laughed.

"Ouch, let me guess, stumbled into the wrong class and Ajax decided to enrol you into his?" Ophelia guessed.

"You got it, how come you and Eric call Mr. Adler by his name?" Liv asked both Eric and Ophelia.

Both of them turned to one another and laughed.

"Let's say we know him on a personal level." Eric laughed.

89

"Hey Eric, you should invite her over, dad will love her." Ophelia

suggested.

"Well actually we were going to mine today to finish of this English

project then we were going to go your place some other time. Right

Eric?" Liv nudged.

Eric nodded with a face filled with a BLT sandwich.

"Well, I best be going still got chemistry, see you soon Liv." Ophelia

smiled, as she hugged Liv and disappeared to her next lecture.

Chapter Seven

After Ophelia left, Liv and Eric were alone. Something felt off, but she couldn't quite put her finger on it. Liv finished her part of the sandwich and grabbed a drink. Her mother always moaned that she didn't drink enough.

"So, what you want to do? I have a gap now until home time, but we have to fill them up with extra- curricular activities, so our minds don't turn into mush." Eric laughed.

"I think I might just go home actually, not feeling too great." Liv replied.

She was unsure why she was feeling unwell, maybe Eric decided to

poison her she wondered, half-jokingly but with a genuine seed of doubt.

Slowly easing herself to her feet, she could hear music in the distance.

"Hey Eric, do you hear that?" Liv asked inquisitively.

Eric looked confused at Liv. Nothing was playing, it was quiet where

they were which is why Ophelia and Eric usually ate lunch there.

"No, I don't hear anything. You okay Liv?" Eric asked with concern.

Tuning into the strange melody, Liv could hear it as clear as day. She got

up and followed the tune.

The music playing was very distinctive to her, almost familiar, however,

she could have sworn she had never heard the tune before.

Losing concentration on where she was actually going, Liv found herself

away from the Academy and somewhere in a dark alley.

The alley was tight, enough for one person to walk though, the walls

were slightly damp and smelt like the bins that were placed up against

them. Looking around, Liv was alone; Eric was nowhere to be seen and

Liv had no clue how she got there. There was a glimpse of light at the

end of the alley. Walking towards it, Liv had one feeling deep in her

stomach which made her feel uneasy: Fear. The houses that towered

above the alley had created a looming shadow that reduced any light

from entering the alley.

All of a sudden, there was a bump. Someone had walked into the bins.

Looking halfway down the alley from where she was at, Liv stared at the

mysterious figure who was standing there.

From what Liv could make out it was a male. Hunched over he looked

like he was hurt or just about ready to run. Liv couldn't make out his

93

face, the shadows around the alley were also cast over him. However, his stature seemed abnormally tall and his was built. Starting to shuffle in a disoriented, zombie-like motion the male figure grew closer to Liv.

In a panic, Liv broke out into a run, her breath was ragged, and she could hear behind her the loud thuds of footsteps. Liv burst through the alley, but the figure had caught up with her, pinning her to the wall and sniggering.

As Liv was about to scream for help, she was disturbed by a knocking sound on what seemed to be a door.

Gasping like all the air had been sucked out of her, Liv frantically looked around to find herself in a toilet cubicle. The knocking continued and she could hear a familiar voice this time.

"Olivia, are you okay? I don't think it was a good idea for you to be here any longer." The voice sounded worried.

Stepping out of the cubicle, Liv was faced with Eric, and she could hear student voices outside the toilet. Confused on where she was, she turned to Eric.

"What just happened?" She asked, trembling a little.

"You had got up from lunch and said you weren't feeling well, we both walked together towards the English lecture room as it was free then you started running and came in here. I thought you needed to be sick or something." Eric explained gently.

Liv caught a glimpse of herself in the mirror behind him, her forehead was clammy and the foundation under her eye had started to reveal the purple bruise under her eye socket.

95

"So how come you're in the ladies' room?" Liv asked in a playful tone.

She could see that Eric was worried, so she attempted to lighten the

mood. Looking at Liv Eric seemed to hesitate, his face started to turn a

little pinkish.

"Er...Well... You were in here for a while..." Eric began.

"Pervert." Liv laughed winking at him.

"Hey! I'm not a pervert I was really worried about you!" Eric exclaimed,

trying to hide the embarrassment written all over his face.

Liv giggled and shoved him through the door towards the corridor.

"Only teasing, come on let's go." She giggled.

Liv still was feeling ill from what happened. She couldn't have

hallucinated that, it seemed too real for her.

"Okay, okay, but Liv are you sure you're alright?" Eric asked.

96

"I'm fine. Now let's find somewhere we can study." Liv responded.

She didn't want to tell Eric what had happened, she didn't want him to

think that she was going crazy. A chill shivered down her back as she

tried to remember what the man had looked like. Even when he had

grabbed her Liv couldn't remember how he sounded or even what he

looked like.

Distracted in her own thoughts, Liv could feel her insides turn with

unease. Doing the best, she could, Liv ignored the feeling and focused on

studying.

Approaching their English room, Eric opened the door.

"Ladies first." He teased.

Rolling her eyes playfully, Liv walked in and sat down in her usual seat.

"Right, time to fully organise what we are going to talk about first." Liv

spoke, determined that they will both defeat the project.

"Sounds like a plan," Eric smiled.

Looking at all their notes sprawled across the table, Olivia started to

rearrange them in chronological order.

"Have you got a laptop on you? If we do this as a presentation it would

be much easier." Liv suggested.

Nodding in agreement Eric reached behind into his blue rucksack and

pulled out a top of the range Apple Mac.

"You know how to operate one of these?" Eric asked.

Liv was taken aback at how fancy his laptop looked compared to her

first-generation, second-hand Mac she had got for her birthday from her

grandparents.

98

"Yeah, I have one similar, however it's not as flashy as yours." Liv

replied.

Sliding the laptop towards her Eric started to make a start on his notes.

Liv opened PowerPoint onto his Mac and started to lay out what their

project was going to look like.

"So, what are we going to do in terms of talking?" Eric questioned.

"Well, I was thinking you could do most of the explaining since this is

your area and I'll explain the bits I definitely know." Liv suggested,

chasing her fingers across the desk.

"Okay, you can talk about the themes of tragedy, romance, and love then.

I'm definitely an expert." Eric teased and copied Liv, sprawling his arms

across the table.

99

"Ha, funny you should say that. I have never been in love, so I wouldn't know how it feels." Liv trailed off.

Looking in surprised Eric shook his head and used one of his hands to play with his hair.

"Wow, really that kinda sucks but in a way its good too." Eric reassured.

"Have you ever been in love? What does it feel like" Olivia asked.

"Well… yes, I have been, a long time ago, I suppose it feels like all the air from a room has been sucked out and only they have it." He began, sitting up from his slouch.

"It's cliché I know, but the energy within you becomes hot as you feel the passion for that person running in your blood." He continued. As Liv was listening to Eric softly brushed her arm with his fingertips. He leaned in closer to her. Liv pulled away flustered slightly. Feeling like electricity had sent 40,000 volts through her, Liv blushed as she could

feel her heart pounding against her ribcage. "Love is like electricity

running through your body, is a smoke and is made with the fume of

sighs." Eric smiled as he leaned towards Liv.

Liv got up and dodged his almost kiss.

"You stole that off Shakespeare!" Liv laughed.

Ignoring his most brutal, -and first- rejection Eric threw his hands in the

air.

"By the gods! She's learned it!" Eric laughed with her reaching into his

pocket.

"Gods…GODS! Shoot I'm supposed to do an assignment that Ms.

Aumont set me!" Liv cried.

"it'll be fine! I'll tell you what, you can borrow my laptop for the assignment you've got to do now I have to go sort something out." Eric offered pulling his phone out.

"Are you sure? That's really kind of you." Liv replied.

Eric got up from his chair and started to walk down the stairs from the aisle they were sat in.

"Meet you by the bus stops, and we'll finish this at yours." Eric added.

Liv nodded in response as she watched Eric disappear out of the room.

The room was as silent as the dead, when Eric left. Liv started to feel uneasy again as her stomach began to twist. Looking around and then back to Eric's Mac, she started on her assignment, researching in depth about the golden apples and how they granted immortality to a god that had consumed one with the approval of Idun.

102

An hour had passed, and Liv had almost completed the essay. Out of

boredom mixed with a little hint of innocent curiosity, Liv decided to

snoop around on Eric's Mac.

Her heart sank, as she scrolled through his photos that revealed

something that Liv wished she had never found.

Chapter Eight

Disappointment filled Liv's heart. That and betrayal. For someone who dared to flirt with her then have tried to kiss her! She was not okay with the picture she had found at all.

On the dreaded Mac screen was a picture of Eric embracing a girl who look liked Catherine.

Catherine looked completely different to what she did now.

Her slutty outfits where swapped out for modest and elegant ones. Her face didn't have a single trace of makeup and her hair was put up in a tidy bun.

For a second Liv pitied Catherine as she clearly was in love with Eric.

However, it did make her wonder why Eric had lied to her in the first

place and what he said to make her so upset.

Replaying the conversation about being in love, Liv realised that Eric

had mentioned that he had been in love before. Could it possibly? No,

Liv thought, she couldn't get past that he had lied to her. After

everything, she couldn't believe her eyes.

"Why are you in this lecture room?" A blunt and authoritative voice

asked.

Liv snapped up to see Ms. Aumont glaring at her from across the room.

"I wanted to get on with your assignment." Liv replied, jumping at the

sound of her voice.

Ms. Aumont narrowed her eyes and walked towards Liv.

105

"I see, you're the mystery girl that is hounding my son." She added

pointing at Eric's laptop.

Quickly closing down the lid she sighed and started to pack her things

away.

"I am not hounding him, my English teacher put us together for a

project." Liv huffed.

"Oh, Ajax did? I'll have a word with him. If you knew what was best,

stay away from a man who is engaged with another woman." Ms.

Aumont threatened.

Feeling a hot burning sensation feeling Liv got up and faced her lecturer.

"You know what. Tell your son to stay away from me then and he can

have this back too." Liv snapped, shoving the Mac in Ms. Aumont's

arms.

106

Speechless and somewhat pleased Ms. Aumont nodded and watched Liv

storm off.

"Huh, that girl has some courage after all." She pondered.

She admired the guts Liv to make a stand and prove she has a backbone,

so much so she even smiled wryly to herself in fusion of bemusement

and pride.

In all her years, Liv was the first student that dared to stand up against

Ms. Aumont, with that Ms. Aumont felt nothing but respect for Liv.

*

*

Liv, marched her way through the university. She had made her way out

of the school grounds. The need to escape had lingered for a while, since

she found out Eric was engaged.

Waving down the next bus she could find, she decided to explore the

town.

Then her phone went off.

Message: From Eric

Where are you? and why has my mum got my laptop?

Making her way to the back of the bus Liv angrily tapped on her phone:

Why did you lie to me about Catherine? Oh, and forgot the part you were

ENGAGED.

108

Punching the send button Liv jiggled her legs waiting for his excuse.

Message: From Eric

I can explain later please don't get mad over it, it was a VERY, long time

ago…

Ghosting his pathetic final excuse of a message, Liv shoved her phone

into her pocket and ignored it for the rest of the journey. As she stepped

off the bus Liv browsed the shops looking for any kind of retail therapy

that would calm her down. As her anger faded the feel of unease

swarmed her. Walking cautiously past one of the shops, Liv stopped and

stared at an alley way that was conveniently right opposite. The shadows

danced in the alley, just as they did in Liv's imagination, all that she

needed now was… Wait… In the shadows Liv could just make out a hooded man. Hunched over like before, he looked like as if he was

waiting for her to approach.

Dodging the alley, at all costs Liv ducked into one of the shops to avoid

the hooded figure. Poking her head out of the doorway, Liv could see the

weather turn; the bright blue sky, now a dulling grey with blackened coal

clouds, lead to a sense of trepidation. She needed to take care.

Looking at her phone, she realised she had been there for an hour and

decided to catch the bus back home, unaware that the strange, hooded

figure had disappeared from the alley.

Waiting at the bus stop, Liv had her headphones in listening to Poisoned

Heart by The Ramones. As she continued listening, the bus rolled up

screeching its breaks to a halt. Little did Liv realise some one was behind

her. Instead of sitting at the back of the bus Liv sat near the front.

Making herself comfortable the hooded figure also boarded the bus.

Chills shot up Liv's spine as she watched him walk past her and park

directly right behind her.

Pausing her music, Liv could feel the hairs on her neck stand up. She

didn't look back as she didn't want to acknowledge that he was sat right

behind her. Thinking fast, Liv thought if she used the buses window

reflection she could see if he was actually sitting right behind her. Her

heart was racing as she slowly shifted her eyes towards the window. The

important thing she had to remember was not react suddenly.

As she glanced at the window, she could see a hooded disturbing figure

sat right behind her. Liv could feel the blood in her body run cold as she

started to feel dizzy and uneasy. Sweat started to bead against her

forehead. She needed to calm down or she would potentially risk herself

111

getting hurt. Squeezing her eyes shut, she pressed resume and continued listening to the Ramones. A bus journey had never felt so long in Liv's life.

Thinking to herself, if she got off at the bus stop by her house, the hooded figure would figure out where she lived. Hating the fact, she was about to do it Liv opened her eyes and launched her messages app on her phone.

Meet me off the bus in about 5 mins, I think someone is following me…

She pressed send and prayed she'd get an answer.

Her phone was silent with no reply or any trace from the recipient.

Liv could feel her eyes getting heavy and her head started to pound. She thought to herself that a panic attack could happen any moment if she didn't remain calm.

Throughout the longest five minutes of her life, Liv tried to convince herself that the man behind her was just a coincidence and that maybe he just wanted to get a seat close to the front too.

Liv also tried to convince herself that it wasn't a man sat behind her, just a woman that was wearing a hood due to the rain that was approaching. Unfortunately, as much as Liv wanted to believe that scenario all she could smell was aftershave, indicating that the person behind her was in fact male.

Her heart still pounded against her chest as she couldn't help but think about her hallucination in the alley way. Looking out the window, desperately avoiding eye contact with the hooded figure's reflection, Liv

could see the University in the distance. Reiterating inter head, almost

like a mantra, how she was going to calmly get off the bus and not run

into the university, Liv could feel herself feeling more at ease as she

could see the university drawing closer.

Pressing the STOP button Liv calmly got up from her seat and walked

towards the doors of the bus. Eyes followed her as she got up and walked

away. All Liv could think in that moment was, don't look back, don't

look back'. As the bus abruptly stopped the doors flung open. Liv again,

calmly stepped off the bus and made her way towards the university.

Her breath was staggered, and her sight began to fuzz. As the bus drove

off, she spun back and saw that the hooded figure had disappeared. The

fact he didn't get off the bus confused Liv. She couldn't have made that up she felt his presence right behind her as if he was almost quite literally breathing down her neck.

Looking around, Liv could only see blurs of other students getting ready to go back to their homes. The outside of the uni was filled with students and lecturers rushing to get as far away from the place as possible.

Few students pushed past Liv unknowingly. As she slightly lost her footing, she continued to walk into the door. Liv quickly grabbed the railing that was supporting her to get into the foyer. She could feel her chest getting tighter, as she knew that this was a belated panic attack that she restrained from having on the bus stop.

Liv started to hear white noise in her ears as it buzzed at an excruciating high pitch. Liv tried to cover her ears as she could see a blur of a figure running towards her.

She couldn't make out what they were saying, but she heard them muffling words that she could not make out. Only low noises that sounded almost like a semblance of a voice. Liv felt herself falling, as a pair of strong muscular arms had caught her from her fall. Looking up squinting she could see the outline of an angelic face with dark raven hair.

"Eric…" Liv whispered.

Then it all went black.

Chapter Nine

Slowly opening her eyes, Liv started to come around. She couldn't tell

where she was. Moving her head, she realised she was sat up with a

jumper as a pillow.

"Hey, you're awake, you scared me back there." A voice softly spoke

beside her.

Liv sat up realising she was in a car. Looking to her she saw Eric; his T-

shirt was tightly fit, and his beautiful flawless hair was an absolute state.

She studied his face, and she could see it was full of worry. As mad as

Liv wanted to be at Eric, she knew that she couldn't stay mad at him. He

probably had a good reason for lying to her, after all.

117

"Where are you taking me?" Liv croaked.

"Back to yours. Penny told me where you live so I thought you could rest up somewhere comfortable." Eric calmly explained.

"Thank you, Eric." Liv replied almost whispering.

Eric looked at her briefly as he half smiled back.

"You want to tell me what that text you sent me was about?" Eric asked raising an eyebrow.

Liv shook her head dismissively. She tried to think of what happened, but her mind was all fuzzy like an old TV with no signal.

"Okay then, I'm surprised you did message me- I thought you hated me."

He replied, looking saddened as he concentrated on the road ahead.

Liv remained silent. Feeling slightly guilty that she had sent him the

passive aggressive text messages.

She looked out the window to see that they were passing the shop where

Liv first met Eric and his family.

"So, what does your dad do?" Liv asked suddenly, thinking that she had

not yet met him.

"He's a doctor, works at the local hospital, it's quite near to your place I

think." Eric replied.

"Think your place is coming up." He added as he started to break and

pull into Liv's driveway.

"Thanks for helping me today I really appreciate it." Liv smiled as she

started to open the door.

119

"Wait a second let me get that for you." Eric quickly spoke with a matter of urgency.

He swiftly got out of his car and opened the car door for Liv. He slipped his arm around her waist and placed his hand on the small of her back, supporting her to her front door. Liv tried swatting him away not realising how weak her legs were from her panic attack.

Grabbing her keys, she unlocked the front door as they both walked through. Guiding Liv through her house Eric led to her room.

"Nice place you've got here." Eric complimented, placing her down onto her bed.

"Thanks, it's not bad for student accommodation. Would you like a drink or something?" Liv asked.

120

She tried to get up however Eric placed his hand gently on her shoulder.

"I think it's best that you rest, tell me where the kitchen is, and I'll get

you something for dinner." Eric replied helpfully.

"Look I'm fine, you don't need to nurse me." Liv lowered her voice,

slightly embarrassed that Eric had offered to cook in her own home.

"Trust me it's the least I can do, since I kinda caused this mess." Eric

sighed.

Liv felt an empty pit in her stomach that kept getting deeper every time

Eric decided to do something nice for her.

Liv didn't reply to that remark and instead gestured to where the kitchen

was. Eric smiled and made his way there, leaving her alone in her

bedroom.

Liv started to feel uneasy. As she shut her eyes, she could start to picture

the hooded man. Her eyes snapped open.

"Eric, I'm coming to keep you company." Liv shouted through the

house.

She slowly got up from her bed and started to pad at the ground with her

feet to see if she could make it. She stood up from her bed, using any

surface she could find to support her she made her way to the kitchen.

Eric was busy running around the kitchen cooking things.

"Where did you get these fresh veggies from? I swore I only had junk in the cupboards." Liv confusingly asked.

Eric looked up at her and laughed.

"I had some veggies with me from home, as I thought you would have just brought junk food." He chuckled.

"I didn't know that you were such a chef." Liv teased.

"Well, don't hold onto that until you've tasted what I made you it could be awful for all I know." Eric chuckled once again.

Washing up as he was going along, Eric glanced at the photo that Liv had left by her sink.

"Parents I assume?" he asked.

Liv looked at the picture that she loathed so much and frowned.

"Speaking of photos what's the deal with the one with you and Catherine? And yes, they are unfortunately." Liv challenged.

Holding a spatula in one hand and raising the other free hand in defeat Eric huffed.

"I suppose you deserve the answer." He mumbled.

Clearly this was a subject that he didn't really like talking about, but he started it first Liv thought to herself.

"As you probably could tell the Catherine I knew back then was different to the bitchy one you know now. My mother and her mother and father were very close as we were growing up. Both coming from quite well-off families our parents had arranged for us to be together." Eric started to explain.

Taking out a tray of freshly made lasagne he started to dish it up.

124

"So, we were joined at the hip, we went through school together until now. We were in love for a short time when I had to propose to her, however that's when the sweet girl I knew became the girl you know today. We used to argue a lot as she wanted to be married ASAP, whereas I wanted to be sure. During this time, her mother and father got divorced and her mother remarried Penny's son. Catherine became obsessed with popularity in fear her mother would push her away as her father did. Then the day I saw you waving at my sister at the supermarket I knew I couldn't cope with the engagement and broke it off. As you can tell my mother isn't the best pleased with my decision." Eric continued to explain.

Liv was overwhelmed by how much pressure Eric had been put under.

Sliding her a plate Eric smiled.

"Now you know the full story." Eric laughed, serving himself some of his masterpiece.

"That must have been really hard on you, but I'm glad you didn't make that silly mistake. Besides, aren't you far too young to marry yet?" Liv laughed trying to lighten the mood.

"What about you then? What's with the only family photo that's here and not in your bedroom?" Eric asked.

Liv looked down and grabbed a chair to sit on. Scooping some of the lasagne she took a bite of it. Deliciously mouth- watering she thought.

"Well, my parents don't really contact me since I moved here… My old

uni was really nice, they just didn't want to pay for all the tuition fees."

Liv began.

Eric stared at her intensely studying every word of her life story.

"So yeah, my parents are stupidly rich too, however I don't see a penny

of it as they want me to earn my place in the big real world. To be honest

with you, I think they are glad to see the back of me." Liv rolled her eyes

and finished.

"What were your parents' names again?" Eric asked.

"Karen and Richard Osmund… Why do you ask?" Liv shot back.

"Oh yes, the Osmund's. My family met them at a party not so long ago

and they were talking how much they could use a better uni for their

daughter…" Eric trailed off.

127

"So, you had something to do with me being able to get in the uni without having a single penny on me." Liv exclaimed.

Eric nodded as he shovelled his part of lasagne into his mouth.

As the late afternoon soon turned into evening both Liv and Eric spent the whole time in the kitchen getting to know each other.

"Favourite colour?" Liv quizzed

"Blue. Favourite song?" Eric asked back

"I would say I Started Something I Can't Finish by The Smiths, but I found a new tune that just is tranquil I don't know the name of it just that some kid at uni plays it occasionally." Liv replied.

The corners of Eric's mouth turned into a mixture of a playful smile and a smile of appreciation.

"Ooh maybe this mystery piano man is the man of your dreams." Eric

teased.

"I didn't say it was on the piano." Liv flirted.

Eric stiffened and his cheeks hushed a slight pinkish to them.

"You're the one who plays it aren't you?" Liv asked.

"Okay you win. I do play piano often but that song you love is actually

an original piece." Eric smiled trying to shake off his embarrassment.

"Knew it." Liv whispered victoriously.

Checking the time, the clock on her wall read 8:30PM

"It's getting pretty late I should probably go back." Eric whispered

clearing up the dishes and picked Liv up who still wasn't fully recovered.

As he picked her up Liv wrapped her arms around him. Her fingers playing with the hair at the back of his neck. He looked at her and

smiled.

"Stop that it tickles." He laughed lowly.

Liv giggled as he gazed into her eyes protectively as he placed her into

her bed. Letting go of him Liv got herself comfortable.

"You're okay now I think." Eric smiled, checking over her.

Suddenly the rain had started to pitter patter on the roof of the house.

"There's a storm inbound tonight look after yourself." Eric cautioned. He

leaned over her to give her a kiss on her forehead but stopped himself

and started to turn away.

Remembering how bad the weather was when the hooded man was

around Liv suddenly grabbed Eric's arm.

"Please don't leave me tonight." Liv trembled.

Her eyes full of fear as she didn't feel safe knowing that she had been

followed. Eric turned back to her and nodded.

"Okay, only for tonight, you've been through a lot today." He replied.

Kicking his shoes off he sat on top of the covers with Liv and slid his

arm behind her head. Liv snuggled into his chest as she fell asleep.

Chapter Ten

Sunshine woke Liv up that morning. She stirred in her bed until she realised that what she was resting her head on was soft but harder than her pillow. She opened her eyes wondering what the curious thing she was lying on was. Looking down she could see her jeans, which indicated to her that she didn't get ready for bed, and she also noticed an extra pair of legs.

Liv very slowly tilted her head upwards to notice a sleeping, Eric. She blushed fiercely as she couldn't believe that she had let a guy stay in her room all night!

132

Feeling all flustered, Liv got up. Checking her phone, she realised that today was a day off from uni. She flipped her head back towards Eric, who was sleeping soundly. Liv had never seen him look as peaceful yet exhausted as he did.

Recalling to last night's events, Liv had remembered that she had asked Eric to stay with her. Feeling selfish from her actions, Liv decided to tuck Eric in so he could get some proper rest. His hair flopped over his face as he stirred whilst Liv try to gently move him. Watching over him lie a subdued guardian angel she brushed his hair out of his face gently. After Liv had tended to Eric, she made her way to the kitchen to make herself something to eat. She felt much better, but she didn't know what came over her when she had asked Eric to stay the night.

133

As she was making herself breakfast, a buzz came from her pocket:

Message From: UNKNOWN NUMBER:

Heyya Liv! I hope you're feeling better Eric had told me you were shook

up yesterday and gave me ya number. Hope you don't mind

-Fi oxo

Liv smiled at her phone. She loved Ophelia, her high energy and

bubbly personality was infectious, a pleasant change from all the

dourness and drabness she'd found herself immerse in since moving.

Liv texted back:

No problem at all! If ur wondering where Eric is, he's over at my

place, he looked after me last night.

134

Send.

Liv left her phone on the side as she started eating the waffles that

she had toasted. Next thing she knew her phone started to ring.

"OH MY GOD TELL ME EVERYTHING" A voice hollered down

the line as Liv answered it.

"Shh, you'll wake him yelling like that." Liv whispered then giggled.

"Sooo what happened? Don't tell me that pervert tried to sleep with

you! Low blow from bro." Ophelia energetically asked.

"No, he didn't! Literally we weren't even undressed or even in bed

properly. Plus, I don't think Eric is like that." Liv assured.

Laughter started to echo down Liv's phone.

"Hahaha, Eric is the biggest perv going! I've snooped in his room!"

Ophelia chuckled.

"You're his sister, of course you'll think that! Besides, he's not a

pervert." Liv denied.

"Who's a pervert?" Yawned Eric stretching his arms.

"No one! Just an er, prank call!" Liv jumped, quickly hanging up her

phone.

Eric leant with his arm draped nonchalantly against the door frame

and raised an eyebrow. His hair was a bedhead mess, but damn he

looked hot! Liv thought. She bit her lip and could feel herself

blushing.

136

Eric smiled devilishly as he started to approach Liv. She edged away

as she knew exactly what he was going to do. Eric pounced as he

blocked Liv from escaping. Doing the foolish thing, Liv ran straight

into Eric as he twirled her around back into the place she started.

"I win." He grinned smugly.

"How did you?" Liv asked confused what he meant.

Holding his hand up revealing his victory Liv's jaw dropped.

"How'd you steal my phone." She gasped.

"With ease. Don't worry, I could tell by your shhing earlier it was Fi.

She always calls me a perv." He smiled, facepalming.

Liv looked impressed by the way Eric had guessed in one go that

Ophelia was on the phone. She held her hand out and gestured to hand it over. With compliance Eric did as she asked and placed her

phone into her hand.

"Oh! I got something for you, let's call it an apology gift from me on

behalf of how my mother acted." Eric suddenly remembered.

"Wait here."

Liv nodded as Eric walked out the door towards his car. Liv followed

to the doorway and watched him rummage through the stuff in his

car everything from CD's to random receipts.

"Found it! Here, this is for you I know you like your mythology so I

thought this would be fitting." Eric smiled.

Walking back, he handed over a rectangular purple velvet box.

"Thank you but you didn't need to buy me anything." Liv replied

gratefully, her cheeks reddening in coy nervousness.

She opened the box to it reveal an 18-karat gold necklace. The chain

was an illustrious gold and so was the pendant on it. It was the shape

of an apple, with a single diamond that was placed in one of the

corners of the apple.

"This is beautiful. But I couldn't take something as precious as this."

Liv replied, overwhelmed by the gift.

"Oh sh, you're the one thing in this room that I can see that's

precious." Eric replied casually.

Liv blushed at the compliment, placed the necklace on the table and

bunched her hair up.

"Help me put it on then." Liv smiled.

Eric closed the door behind him and assisted Liv with her necklace.

The necklace dazzled with luminous splendour as Eric fastened it

around her neck. He smoothed her hair down and Liv could feel his

breath on the back of her neck.

Goosebumps. The hairs on the back of her neck stood up as Liv

turned to face Eric, longingness and sheer wonder filling her eyes.

She had wanted to kiss him for a very long time and now

she had the chance. She leaned into him, expecting him to do the

same. However, he pulled back.

"Not just yet! Soon we can, I promise." Eric whispered lowly, as if

pulling himself away took all the will in the world.

Liv blushed, embarrassed by her bold move. Supposed she deserved

it as she did the same to him not so long ago.

"How come we have to wait." Liv mumbled lowly with trepidation,

embarrassed by what she had asked as soon as the words left her lips.

"I don't want to rush into things. You already know about Catherine and

how that all turned out. You can probably understand why I want to wait.

It would kill me if I lead you on." Eric explained.

Liv looked down feeling guilty and highly embarrassed.

"I understand." Liv sighed.

Eric grabbed her hands reassuringly and smiled.

"Believe me, I want to so bad. It takes a lot of resistance for me to hold back." Eric reassured and shot a wink at her.

Liv thought about what Eric had said hard. As he was standing there, Liv could imagine her angel and devil on her shoulder. The angel was telling her to respect his wishes and wait for the right time. Whereas the devil was telling her to play, and tease him until he gave in.

Liv shot back a playful smile as she stepped towards Eric.

Eric stiffened as she approached him.

"So, what you are saying is that I am almost irresistible?" Liv teased as she circled him.

Like a lion challenging another lion.

"Well…" Eric began to think, before he tried to think of something else.

142

Liv giggled softly as she ran her fingers up Eric's shirt. His abs were chiselled, and she could feel him tense.

Eric's face was tinted pink as Liv wound him up. With any semblance of willpower, he had draining from him, he pulled her hands out from underneath his top flipped her around and held her hips.

"Stop it, you don't want to play this game with me. You know I will win." He whispered into her ear.

His words sent prickles up her neck, as she knew that she had stumbled on making the wrong decision.

Trying to flip herself to face him, Eric held her hips forward restricting

her to turn around. He then brushed his lips against her collar bone and

made his way to her neck.

Liv tilted her head back beckoning him to continue.

A low laugh came from behind her as Eric released her.

"Told you I would win." Eric laughed hysterically.

Liv playfully punched him.

"Wow, your sister is right! You ARE a pervert after all." Liv laughed

back.

Eric raised his brow becomingly and jabbed her in the sides.

"Speaking of my sister, we are going into town along the pier to our favourite spot if you'd like to join us. Besides, once I tell Fi, you don't get a choice and will have to come with us."

"Fine- only if you do some of our English Project first. Then we'll talk about it." Liv smiled.

Chapter Eleven

As the afternoon turned into evening, Liv still was feeling a little

flustered with her actions earlier on.

"What time are we going?" Liv asked.

"Soon- just got to freshen up and wait for Fi to get back to me." Eric

replied.

"Well, I'm going to pick out something nice to go out in. Which means

my room is out of bounds." Liv giggled.

"Right, shall I freshen up first since you'll only make us late?" Eric

joked.

Liv opened her mouth in shock, and huffed she marched past him.

146

"I'll show you!" She exclaimed.

Eric laughed as Liv entered her room, slamming the door behind her in faux outrage and letting out a long exhale.

Eric had gotten into her head and she needed to focus on her outfit to take her mind off this morning.

Quickly prancing to her wardrobe, Liv sifted through the numerous outfits that she could wear. Unfortunately, Liv wasn't the greatest on dressing to impress Eric as well as dressing appropriately for dinner. Lost in thought of what she was going to wear, there was a knock on her bedroom door.

"Hey Liv, you're proving my point- but seriously you need to hurry Fi is almost in town." Eric announced.

"Oh sorry! Just give me a min!" Liv called through the door.

Starting to panic, she whipped her phone out and started frantically

tapping;

Hey Fi, I need help ASAP Wardrobe CRISIS! If ur on the bus stay on and

meet me at my house NOW. Xo.

She paced impatiently, wiggling her phone between her palms until she

got a response…

Message From: Fi

ON MY WAY!!

Liv sighed with relief; she didn't really get along with females. However,

she was grateful that Fi had befriended her.

After a few minutes, there was a knock at the front door.

"Eric, could you get that please?" Liv called.

Hearing the door open Liv assumed he obeyed.

148

"Outta the way brother EMERGENCY!" Fi exclaimed barging past Eric.

"Wait what!? Hey, Liv are you okay?!" Eric called, trying to follow Fi to

Liv's bedroom.

"I'm fine, let Fi come in, stay out there. Girl stuff!" Liv shouted back to

him.

Liv could hear Eric sigh with relief assuming he made himself

comfortable. Fi entered Liv's room.

"So... what do you need help with to impress my brother?" Fi teased

coyly.

"This is why I love you. You know, that right?" Liv laughed.

Fi stepped into the wardrobe and sifted through the outfits that Liv held

in her possession.

"Right, I'm guessing you don't socialise much, try this and this oh and this! It's MEGA cute!" Fi excitedly directed. Rambunctiously pulling outfit after outfit from Liv's wardrobe, bundling them all into her arms.

Liv stripped out of her clothes she was wearing and slid into the outfit that was 'mega cute'. The outfit was a black velvet dress with lacy bits that came down to her knee.

"I'm not sure about this. It seems too slutty. We aren't dating…" Liv hesitated.

"Yet." Fi shot back.

Both of them started giggling which alerted Eric's attention.

"Hey, can you BOTH hurry up now." Eric called his tone growing impatient.

"Right NEXT!" Fi demanded.

150

The second outfit was a little more toned down, it was a jumpsuit that

was black and had sunflowers on it.

"I think that's a little too conservative for you." Fi chipped in.

"I kinda like it…" Liv trailed off.

Fi looked through the outfits that she had picked out for Liv and thought

hard.

"Okay this one is definitely THE ONE." Fi laughed.

Liv gasped the dress that Fi picked out was a skater dress that resembled

a sailor dress. What Fi didn't know is that this was the dress she was

wearing in the horrible family photo.

Shrugging that thought out of her head, Liv decided to try it on in the en

suite bathroom of hers. She closed the door and slipped the dress on,

brushing her tangled hair to smooth it out.

"Fi, can you call Eric in here?" Liv asked.

"Eric you've been granted access!" Fi bellowed.

"Finally, what took you so-"

Liv stepped out of the bathroom; Eric's eyes were glued to her leaving

him speechless.

"Wow, you look beautiful Liv." Eric continued, clearing his throat.

"Thank you this was my genius work, I'm hungry let's get some grub!"

Fi intervened.

Fi led the way followed by Liv then Eric.

*

*

Arriving at the local restaurant, Liv and Fi got out while Eric went to find somewhere to park. Entering the restaurant for the first time Liv was in awe. The setting was calm and very white; every piece of furniture, wall and floor was all white.

"Have I died?" Liv asked jokingly.

"Nope you're still here thankfully." Eric's voice chuckled from behind them.

"It's quite heavenly, don't you think Eric." Fi remarked shooting a glance at Eric.

Judging on the comment Fi made, it seemed Eric felt uncomfortable.

"So… I'm guessing you're not big on religion?" Liv asked

"You could say something like that." Eric replied.

His expression softened as he guided the ladies to sit down at a table.

"I think it would be waaaay easier if we were religious. Though it does

mean no sex before marriage." Fi trailed off.

Liv flushed and quickly looked away from Eric.

"How about you? Tell us more about you Liv? We don't really know you

all that well," Eric quickly interjected.

"Well, I lived with my parents when I was at my old uni, but I really

wanted to go here. My parents didn't want to pay for tuition, so I had to

earn it and pay for all my accommodation and enrolment myself." Liv

explained.

"So. are your parents rich? Ohh, do they have a boat? We should ride on it?" Fi excitedly asked.

"Me and my parents don't really see eye to eye, if I'm honest."

"Oh, we know about not getting on with family, well how about we steal it!" Fi exclaimed.

Liv laughed at the comment, ordered her food and drink.

"What are you guys getting? I bet Fi you're a burger kinda girl and Eric is a steak kinda guy." Liv beamed.

"Actually, you are wrong, Fi is more of a 'carbie' as she calls it and I prefer salads for dinner." Eric smiled.

"Oh, right that's a surprise to me since I've seen you demolish many a burger at uni." Liv winked.

Eric's cheeks slowly flushed a warm red.

"So, you like to watch me eat?" Eric teased back, masking the fact he

was embarrassed she knew that.

Before Liv and Eric could flirt some more, they were interrupted by the

sounds of dry heaving from Fi.

"Ew, guys this isn't a date and I'M deffo not a third wheel!" She

exclaimed.

Eric and Liv exchanged a look of admiration then laughed loudly.

As their food arrived, they all continued to joke and laugh with each

other until it started to get dark.

"Hey, do you want us to drop you off back at your place?" Eric asked

Liv.

"No thanks I've ordered a taxi, I should be fine though you two go on

ahead." Liv smiled.

156

"Well, if you're sure… I'm just a little worried." Eric replied.

"I'll be fine." Liv reassured squeezing his arm.

Giving her a once over, Eric was assured enough to leave her to it.

"Come on Fi, let's go." Eric called.

"Hey thanks for tonight I really needed it. Both of you." Liv thanked.

Fi stuck her thumb out and walked towards the car park.

Eric stepped forward and brushed Liv's hair from her face, gazing at her

intensely.

"Anytime, and you really did look outstanding tonight" Eric lowly

spoke.

Liv smiled at him as he pecked her cheek.

"See you soon." Eric waved and parted ways.

Liv turned her back to walk towards a taxi that had just pulled up. Her

breath tightened and her head started hurting. She closed her eyes and

reopened them. To her shock she could see a young girl and boy making

out intensely. Liv shook her head to her eyes she could see herself and

Eric as clear as day. All of a sudden, a bright blue light darted at them

and hit them. Liv winced at the sight of Eric's figure crawling to her

lifeless body. Before she could witness what happened next, everything

went black once again…

Chapter Twelve

Liv opened her eyes, her vision still blurred.

Groaning in pain, she tried to sit up. To her astonishment, she soon came

to realise that this wasn't her bedroom at all. The room she was in was

chic, the walls around her were a warm cream which made her feel calm.

Looking around, Liv couldn't tell whose room she was in. To her right

she could see a wooden dressing table that seemed barely used; on the

wall by it, was a mirror that was rounded at the top and was surrounded

by a brass frame. She lifted the soft duck feathered duvet off her and swung her legs to the side of the bed. As she did this, she became aware

of the sheer size of the bed. It was huge! her legs barely reached the

edge. Liv felt like a small doll in a huge house. After feeling

overwhelmed with the pristine room, a wave of fear flooded her. She

must have been kidnapped ... Or maybe someone had drugged her food.

Nope: without hesitation Liv leaped out of the bed and quickly made a

run for the large brown door handle in front. As she opened the door

ready to run, she came out into a long hallway. Directly in front of her

was some sort of balcony. Filled with trepidation and fearing the worst,

she grasped onto the deep brown banister that protected her. From what

Liv could see, across from her was another row of rooms, which gave her

posh hotel vibes. She turned her head within the direction she was intending on heading, which revealed a long hallway dressed in red carpet and magnolia walls.

She started to walk down the hall, where she was greeted with a familiar melody. She continued to walk but, to her confusion, the music wasn't getting any louder. Walking further down the hall in search of the music, a familiar figure emerged from around the corner.

"Liv! There you are! I was like freaking out that I had lost you!" Fi squealed.

"Fi!? What are you doing here?" Liv asked confusingly.

"I live here duh," Fi laughed.

Sudden realisation was written over Liv's face. Of course! she wasn't kidnapped, she was in the famous Aumont Manor, which explained the huge beds and the opulent room.

"So how did I end up at your house and whose bed is that?" Liv

questioned.

Ophelia's face pretty little face turned with concern. In doing so, Ophelia

had changed from the fun bubbly kid, to a concerned mother. Dare Liv

say, Fi looked like her mother.

"Well… Eric had said this had happened before, and this time you were

lying on the floor and cracked your head open. Our father took a look at

you when we brought you back to the house. The strange thing was that

he couldn't figure how you fell, so hard." Ophelia explained.

Liv looked straight at Fi and realised that she had probably gave her a

fright. Fingering her necklace Liv took a minute to think about what she

was going to say next.

Quickly, she decided to lighten the mood up.

162

"So go on then, whose bed was I in?" Liv playfully smiled, giving Fi a

gentle nudge.

As soon as Liv cracked the joke, the Fi she knew and loved returned.

"Don't worry, we stuck you in mine. Thought, you'd be more

comfortable in there," Fi smirked.

"Are you really sure that you are okay though? I think dad should double

check you and change your bandages." Fi again queried.

Liv gave her arm a little squeeze reassuringly and nodded then reached

for her head, realising that she had bandages wrapped around.

"Where is Eric? I should probably thank him." Liv asked.

Fi shrugged,

"I dunno, he disappears when he gets agitated or upset, usually hiding

away from our mother." Fi laughed.

163

"Oh, so does he not get on with your mum?" Liv asked.

"Not really. Mum is pretty old school and likes tradition, I don't mind it much, but Eric is the eldest, so she expects him to lead the family one day." Fi explained.

Liv looked up to see a family portrait of the four of them.

In the portrait Liv could see Ms and Dr Aumont standing behind a lofty throne like chair with, with Fi sat in it to the side of them was Eric, looking handsome stood next to his father. Their faces all looked forthright and serious, apart from Fi who characteristically was pulling the cheesiest grin. Following the picture, Liv then fixed her eyes on Eric who was a lot younger next to the chair, and his mother with her hand on his shoulder. He looked miserable as sin; however, you could tell he was favoured over his sister by their mother.

164

"Does it not bother you that your mum favours Eric?" Liv questioned.

"Not really, I mean you have her as a teacher, right? You know what she's like sometimes I feel sorry for him." Fi replied sadly.

Liv looked down, remembering how much she disliked him at first, then an overwhelming sense of guilt came over her. He must have so much pressure on him that he couldn't help that he was popular.

"The worst thing about Eric-, is that mother wants him to be engaged to someone who is in a high-class family like ours." Fi added.

And the guilt got worse for Liv. After Fi had mentioned that her heart sank as she knew that she wouldn't ever be seen as worthy in Ms. Aumont's eyes. Fi perceived the depressed look on her friends face and gave her a big hug.

"I wouldn't worry about that too much; Eric is a fighter and always gets

what he wants eventually." Fi smiled reassuringly.

Liv hugged her back.

"Thank you, Fi." She whispered.

"Anytime. Now, you must eat something and get plenty of water in you.

Follow me." Fi beckoned.

Taking Liv's arm, she dragged her to the kitchen.

On their way, they went passed several old paintings that looked like

older members of the family. Going down the stairs the red carpet

followed them and led to the closed door that Fi had stopped at.

"Before we go in, I must warn you, I think everyone might be eating

already." Fi quickly mentioned. Liv tried to squirm away to indicate that making an entrance was a big hell no for her. Fi however, held tight to

her and dragged her forward opening the kitchen door.

Chapter Thirteen

Ophelia dragged Liv into the kitchen, there was low chatter as they

entered which, instantly stopped as they entered.

All eyes were on Liv, looks of confusion were on some of their faces

whilst others were shrouded with concern.

"Olivia, how are you feeling?" A friendly male voice asked.

Looking to where the voice was coming from, a middle- aged man, with

reddish brown hair came towards her. From her memory it was Dr.

Aumont.

"I'm feeling fine thank you. And thank you for seeing to my head

injury." Liv thanked.

"Please call me Asmund." Dr Aumont beamed.

Liv smiled politely and nodded; her eyes shifted around the room until

she caught glimpse of two unfortunate familiar faces…

Sat from across of each other was Dr. Adler and Ms. Aumont.

"Next time you come into the kitchen I expect you to be dressed this is

not a sleepover." Ms. Aumont sternly addressed Liv.

Unaware what she was wearing Liv looked down to see barely anything.

She was wearing a skimpy looking nighty which Liv was certain it was

probably transparent.

"Oh, I – I am sorry Ms. Aumont, I'll get changed right away." Liv

stammered in embarrassment.

She started to shuffle back until she was stopped by something. A hand

gently brushed her shoulder, preventing her from escape.

"I see you've met the family, suppose sooner is better than later." Eric

laughed, standing from behind.

Liv slightly relaxed at his touch then became uncomfortable as Ms.

Aumonts' glare seared straight at her.

Her English lecturer got up and walked over to her and Eric.

"Nice to see you again Liv, I hope you both have been doing that

presentation for me still and not what you kids call studying." Mr. Adler

joked

"All sorted actually Uncle Ajax." Eric smiled victoriously.

"Uncle? As in stole notes in uncle?" Liv questioned.

Eric softly jabbed her as she exposed Eric.

"Oh, didn't you know Liv? The lovely lady who is scowling like there in no tomorrow is my sister." Ajax laughed pointing to Ms. Aumont.

"Also known as my mother." Eric smiled at Ms. Aumont.

Ms. Aumont stood up and walked towards Dr. Aumont, he smiled and wrapped his arm around her waist.

"Oh Liv, its best if you stay here a while until you are fully recovered, from what I could see it was a pretty nasty fall and I don't want you leaving concussed." Dr. Aumont said.

Ms. Aumont darted a sly look to her husband, which Liv noticed but pretended to ignore. Catching her gawking, Ms. Aumont gracefully left the kitchen.

Ajax watched her leave the room and decided to follow her.

"I do apologise for my wife she isn't the easiest person to get along with

I know." Dr. Aumont empathised.

"I don't mind I think she's a very extraordinary lady, I'm honoured to be

taking her class this year." Liv replied gratefully.

Eric smiled down at her and gave her a little squeeze.

"I'll leave you in Ophelia's capable hands. Make sure you watch them,

daughter." Dr. Aumont laughed.

From out of the corner of the room Fi gave her father a salute.

"sir, yes, sir." She exclaimed, making Liv jump.

"Eric if you may, step away from the lady." She asked.

Pushing them apart Fi wriggled her way between Liv and Eric.

Dr. Aumont left the room laughing to himself, as Eric and Fi were

fighting over Liv.

172

"Fi, if I give you £10, will you leave me alone with Liv?" Eric smirked.

"Nope, dad said not to take my eye off either of you so that's that!" Fi

argued.

Liv looked at Fi and was confused by her change of character.

"Hey Fi, how come you are so quiet when everyone is here? I didn't

even notice that you were here still?" Liv asked

"Have you not met my mother!? She's one scary-

"Eerikki I would like a word with you." Ms. Aumont sternly announced

making Fi jump and hide behind Liv.

Eric scowled at the name his mother used and left with her.

Crossing their paths Ajax came back to the kitchen.

"Ophelia, have you got anything better to do than standing around?"

Ajax quizzed her.

173

Fi hissed at him, storming off. Liv attempted to grab her arm but failed

as Fi left.

"So, Liv, how are you settling in at uni?" Ajax asked.

"Not so bad, despite my mix up with classes. I'm really enjoying

mythology at the moment despite how tense it seems." Liv said.

Ajax raised an eyebrow, seeming interested in Liv's studies.

"Oh? What are you studying now? I know a bit of mythology myself,

take a seat?" Ajax offered, extending his arm out to one of the empty

chairs at the table.

Liv took up the offer and sat down across from Ajax.

"At the moment we are learning about Idun and Hel. Interesting story

really." Liv replied, trying not to sound too passionate.

"Oh, Idun and the golden apples. Did you know people believe that Idun escaped Hel by killing herself and reincarnating into a human? She also destroyed the apples apart from one to punish the gods for their greed." Ajax quizzed.

Liv's eyes lit up and realised how knowledgeable Mr. Adler was about mythology.

"Wow, I didn't know that, when I did my research on her it only mentioned that she was killed. But Hel was also daughter of Loki, so she was good at manipulating, who's to say Hel didn't trick Idun to kill herself?" Liv quizzed back lost in her conspiracy.

As she was explaining her theory to Ajax, she was playing with her necklace that Eric had given her, which caught Ajax's attention.

"Say, Olivia, where did you get that necklace?" Ajax asked.

175

His eyes had that glint in them akin to a thief looking at the Queen's

jewels.

"Ajax, it's getting late, probably best to go home and finish your

paperwork?" Dr. Aumont interrupted.

Ajax broke his stare with Liv and got up.

"You're right it is late I best be off." Ajax replied.

"It was nice speaking with you Liv see you in class." Ajax added.

"You too Mr. Adler." Liv replied.

Dr Aumont watched Ajax like a hawk as he left, purveying his every

motion.- He turned to Liv with concern in his expression.

"Don't trust him too much Liv, he's trouble." Dr. Aumont cautioned.

Liv nodded and looked around the kitchen.

"Has Eric finished talking to his mother yet?" Liv asked.

176

"I'm not too sure, probably not my wife likes to lecture our children."

Dr. Aumont replied despondently.

"Pardon me for asking this Dr. Aumont, but why is your wife so cruel?"

Liv asked inquisitively.

Dr. Aumont rubbed the back of his neck and shrugged off his white

doctor's coat and sat next to Liv.

"Since we married… she has been like that. When I first met her, she

was one of the kindest souls I have ever met. Her mother was always

bitter towards me too, so I understand it must be frustrating to you. It

was the way she was brought up by her mother unfortunately. I hope

Ophelia won't be trained the same way; I don't want her to lose her

spirit." Dr. Aumont explained.

As he began talking about his wife, he smiled like a teen who had fallen

in love for the first time, as he explained Ms. Aumonts history his smile

faded.

Liv smiled softly in a reassuring way,

"I don't think you could ever tame Fi." Liv laughed softly.

Dr. Aumont laughed with her as they did Ms. Aumont appeared from the

doorway without Eric.

Chapter Fourteen

Liv looked confusingly at Ms. Aumont in search of Eric.

"If you're looking for my son he's gone." Ms. Aumont abruptly

proclaimed.

"Where." Liv asked shortly.

"I don't know, away from you. Go get dressed." Ms. Aumont snapped

bluntly.

Mr. Aumont looked pained as his wife acted so coarsely towards Liv.

Liv got up from her chair and calmly paced out of the kitchen towards

Ophelia's bedroom.

179

She meandered through the square hall. The carpet was a scarlet red and

complemented the two staircases either side that met to a balcony-

hallway that followed the shape of the hall. Liv grabbed one of the dark

oak banisters and paused.

The sound of sweet soft music rang faintly though the hall. This time,

before she was stopped, Liv decided to follow the musical trail. She

ventured the Aumont manor till she came to a narrow corridor with that

had two entrances to a study and seemed to be a dining room. To her

astonishment, the corridor led to a dead end. The melodic tune was

getting louder towards the dead end. Confused by this Liv begun

venturing down the dead end. Darkness loomed around it as if there was

something to be hidden. Liv continued down the corridor and briefly

paused it looked like a dead end however, the music was still getting

180

louder. Liv reached out and felt the cold wall that was in front of her. It felt cold and slightly damp as if it was a cave wall. Liv pressed her ear to the wall and put her hand on it to keep her steady. All of a sudden there was a clunk and the wall slid to the side, revealing a tight passageway lit by a candle from which the music echoed. The music played loudly almost as if it was beckoning Liv to find it. She shuffled forwards making her way down the tight passage. At the end was a large oak door with a brass handle. Liv placed her hand on the handle, took a deep breath and prepared to be faced what was behind the door.

The door creaked open as the overwhelming melody had been found. Behind the door was a small room. Its black walls and red velvet carpet added to the gothic look of the manor. Surprisingly the room didn't have any electric light but all around the walls were candles cradled in brass holders. Her eyes held the middle of the room. In the middle was where the source of the music was coming from. A grand piano stood proudly in the middle, where a troubled, angry, concerned Eric was sat. Liv had never seen Eric this tranced into his playing he played loudly and fast paced. Liv felt intimidated but also impressed. Until the heavy oak door closed behind her. The music stopped. Eric snapped his head up and looked directly at Liv in surprise.

To her embarrassment Liv quickly whipped around got ready to leave.

"I'm sorry for disturbing you." She quickly mumbled.

"No Liv wait!" Eric shouted.

He shot up and made a run for Liv before she could open the door. As she reached for the door Eric wrapped his long muscular arms around her.

"You found me." He softly whispered.

Liv melted in his arms and paused the freak out she had.

"Where exactly are we? This isn't your Mr. Grey red room is it?" Liv joked.

Eric laughed and took her hand into his.

"No, that's underground." He smirked and shot a wink at Liv.

Liv flushed as she did not expect that answer.

"This is my hideout, I come here whenever I feel stressed, upset or angry, and take my frustration out in my music." Eric explained.

"So, where are we in the mansion?" Liv asked again.

"Between the walls, I discovered this place when I was about 7 playing hide and seek with Fi and my cousins." Eric trailed off.

Liv looked around in awe as she thought it was impressive for a 7-year-old to stumble across a hidden room.

"You said you came here when you are sad or angry. Was it to do with your mother?" Liv questioned with empathy.

"Let's sit down and talk." Eric quickly suggested.

He guided her hand and led her to the piano stool.

"My mother thinks you're trouble that's why she is so cold to you. She's met your parents and because you don't have any money of your own, she thinks you've seduced me to get to my money." Eric explained carefully.

"I've also lied to you Liv. We've met before." Eric added and sighed.

184

Liv's eyes widened and she gasped.

"How? I've never met you?" She replied perplexed with the thought.

"It was just before my parents party they threw, you looked like you had

been drinking with friends and you were alone and sat on the street."

Eric explained.

Liv thought extremely hard to remember that night. And to her

realisation turned fuchsia.

"The first and last night I had blacked out and didn't remember how I got

home." Liv muttered.

"You were crying saying you had to move away but wanted to get into

our uni but didn't have the funds." Eric continued explaining.

"I called a taxi and calmed you down. You were the most beautiful girl I

ever saw. I knew you never felt that way for me though." Eric sighed.

185

"That's a lie. I've never been interested in money. I have always wanted

to find the person and thank them for getting me home safely that night.

And all this time it was you." Liv smiled.

She looked him in the eye and searched for the look that he gave her the

night he stayed. She placed her hand on his cheek and leaned in.

"I do feel something for you Eric and it's powerful." Liv whispered.

She leaned in further and planted a kiss on his lips. Eric relaxed into her

kiss and lingered on her lips as well, his fingers running through Liv's

messy hair as his other hand was placed on the small of her back. As

much as she craved Eric, Liv pulled back.

"Can you hear that?" Liv asked.

"Hear what?" Eric moaned as he planted kisses up and down Liv's neck.

"Footsteps." Liv replied.

Before they could both hear anything, in burst Ophelia with a worried yet

scared look painted on her face.

"Eric. Its dad. Ajax is back with more family." She spoke concerned.

Her voice shook as she used the words dad and Ajax in the same

sentence.

Chapter Fifteen

Eric stiffened and his expression grew cold.

"What do you mean?" He queried lowly.

Ophelia looked as white as a ghost. Her body shook as she opened her

mouth.

"Ajax has attacked dad and brought more family here. They are trying to

find something," Fi trembled.

Eric looked over at Liv, perspiration glinting on his brow, walked over to

his sister.

"We have to stop this. Liv, you need to stay here. It's safe and no one

will find you," Eric instructed.

188

"What? No way! I'm coming with you and Fi!" Liv refused.

"Olivia, you have to stay. They are dangerous people," Fi added, her tone shifted unfamiliarly maternal territory. The assertion in her voice and the anxiousness painted on her face was a blinding contrast from the impish soul Liv had come to know; Fi had never even used Liv's full name before so, something struck fear in her as she did. She knew this was serious.

"Fine," Liv submitted defeat bluntly.

Eric walked back to Liv and pulled her in for a hug.

"Don't worry, I'll be back soon." Eric whispered softy, planting a kiss on her forehead.

Letting go of her like a cliché romance movie, Eric sprinted out of his secret room, leaving Liv behind. The solid oak door started to slowly

189

close off the natural light, and Liv started to think of an opportunity to

help Eric and Fi out.

Liv decided to ignore Eric's instruction and casually walked out like a

disobedient school kid.

After boldly stepping away from the hidden room Liv found herself in

the square hall away from the narrow hallway that led to Eric's secret

room.

A shred of fear ran down her spine as she saw that there were definitely

more people here than there was in the Kitchen. Looking at family

members brawling, Liv caught Fi fighting with a middle-aged man who

was twice the size and heavily built.

Watching them fight was astonishing, like a pair of starving lions

wrangling over the last piece of flesh in the wilderness. At first, Liv thought it was impossible for Fi to even think of taking on a man who was basically looking like The Rock, however Fi's fighting was almost like figure skating, it was so graceful yet unusually powerful... Fi's fist had hooked under the guy's chin and contacted so hard that Liv swore he had been lifted from the floor. Snapping back to reality to where Liv was standing, she had realised that the entire manor resembled a scene from an apocalypse. People were fighting and screaming. It was complete chaos: anarchy.

Liv started to regret her decision to leave the room and the instinct to find Eric to make sure he was safe set in. Liv took an exit and entered the kitchen, dipping and diving through the people who were fighting in the halls.

At the back of the kitchen was a door that led to outside to what seemed the garden. Liv rushed towards the door and left the manor. Outside was completely different to what she imagined it wasn't a garden Liv had stepped into, it was a jungle.

The number of rare flowers, trees and plants that were around really did make a believable jungle.

The path was cobblestone and led up towards some stairs that separated two ways further into the garden and also directly led to a water feature that almost looked like an Amazonian waterfall.

With a wall that ran along the front of it, coming from one of the paths, Liv saw Eric emerge. She started to walk towards him when Ms. Aumont came into view. Liv paused her destination and quickly ducked around the side of the stairs out of sight.

"Eerikki, this is your fault! I told you that you shouldn't have brought

her here!" Ms. Aumont hissed.

Eric scowled at the sound of his full name.

"What was I supposed to do? Let her die in the streets!" Eric spat, getting

into his mother's face.

 Ms. Aumont grabbed Eric by the neck and threw him against the water

feature.

"ITS HER THEY ARE AFTER! IF YOU HAVE FEELINGS FOR HER,

YOU NEED TO END THIS NOW, AS FAR AS I'M CONCERNED,

IT'D BE PREFERABLE IF SHE ENDED UP DEAD," Ms. Aumont

shouted at her son.

Eric kicked her off him and shot a deadly look back at his mother. He

smoothed his damp hair back and smirked.

"Feelings? Pft, I was using her. She was so easy. If you didn't interfere, I could have slept with her and added to my conquests." Eric Slyly laughed.

The words stuck in Liv like tiny daggers in her heart. She should have known; Eric was no different to any other uni guys…

Her eyes felt hot and stingy. Wiping away the tears Liv ran away to collect her things from Ophelia's bedroom.

Bursting into Ophelia's room, Liv put on her old clothes and grabbed her rucksack that she would have taken to uni the next day. As she was about to leave, a beaten-up Fi was at the door.

"Why are you here? Eric told you to stay where it was safe!" Fi Exclaimed.

Liv felt a rage as his name was spoken.

194

"Move out the way Fi, I am leaving. To hell with Eric, he is just an asshole just like every other guy," Liv choked trying to hide how upset she really was.

"You don't mean that- it really isn't a place you want to go… What happened did you two fight?" Fi asked, oblivious to what had happened.

"No, he USED me, Fi! All this time I meant nothing to him. How are you both even so strong? Why are the people downstairs after me?" Liv burst into tears shrieking.

She fell to the ground as she admitted defeat to gravity. Fi knelt beside her and hugged her tightly.

"I'm certain he didn't. I have seen him use girls before… He's different with you, Liv. As for the people who attacked father and are in our house, they are family from my mother and uncle's side of the family. I

195

don't know why they are after you, but you should go back to the room

and talk with Eric. He may help fill the blanks in." Fi explained, wiping

away Liv's tears.

"You really think he isn't using me?" Liv sniffed.

Fi smiled and chuckled.

"If he was, don't you think he would have done so by now?"

Fi was right, that night he came back to her place he had the chance then

but didn't. Liv got up and helped Fi to her feet.

"Where is Eric again? I need to have a serious talk with him," Liv asked.

"He's probably heading back to where YOU should be duh," Fi replied.

Pushing Liv out the door she urged her to go back to find him.

Running through corridors and people still fighting, Liv found her way

safely to the hidden hallway that lead to the room. She opened the door to a frantic Eric looking for her inside. As the door opened, he turned his

head and ran to embrace her.

"Thank the gods you are safe. I told you not to leave." Eric sighed in

relief.

Liv pushed him away

"Explain to me what is going on. I heard you with your mother." Liv

spoke lowly.

Eric gave a look of disbelief then his expression turned serious.

"I know. I saw you leave the door, but I couldn't get rid of my mother I

think she has something to do with dad's attack." Eric explained.

"If you knew I was there, why did you say those hurtful things?" Liv

asked bluntly, annoyance seeping across her face.

Eric looked pained, almost like a wounded animal.

197

"because someone like me isn't to be with someone like you Olivia…"

Eric sighed.

"What do you mean someone like you?" Liv probed again.

"We are descendants of Odin and Hel not demigods, but we inherit

superhuman strength and a few other quirks." Eric explained.

Liv backed up laughing thinking Eric was going crazy.

"That's really funny… please don't joke with me-"

"I'm not joking! The reason Mothers side are after you is because they

are from Hel's side; they think you might be a reincarnated version of

Idun. It's not safe for you here!" Eric snapped.

Liv froze as Eric's words had the hint of panic and fear in them. His

expression read so clearly that Liv knew deep down he was telling the

truth.

198

"Okay. Okay, if this is true… then why is your mother so against us?"

Liv quizzed.

"She thinks that you are bad luck, almost like a bad omen that surrounds

the family, that's why she blames you for dad getting hurt and Ajax

going AWOL. Look, I know we don't have time, but I will explain

everything once this is over.

For now, you really need to stay here. If you ever feel in danger you

need to come here. Only me and Fi know of this place." Eric explained.

The sense of urgency lingered in his voice as he practically begged Liv

to stay out this time.

"No, I won't stay here on my own, I will help fight! I can fend for

myself, and I need to stay with you." Liv argued.

199

Eric sighed, smiled, and took hold of Liv's hands, pressing his forehead

against hers.

"what am I going to do with you huh." He sighed in relief.

He grabbed her hand and admitted defeat, walking out of the room and

towards the door when his mother stood in their path.

"You go I need to talk with my son." Ms. Aumont bluntly spoke to Liv.

Chapter Sixteen

Eric pulled Liv close to him.

"Anything you can say to me you can say to her." Eric hissed.

Liv looked at the death stare that was given towards her and pushed

away from Eric.

"Eric, this is her house. I think we should respect that I'll be over here."

Liv interfered.

Shooting a look back at Ms. Aumont. Amused by her bravery Ms.

Aumont scoffed.

"Now you can stop the act Eerikki, she is no good for you Ajax and the others are going to kill her and if you get in the way you will die too."

Ms. Aumont warned.

"Mothers right in some aspect, there is potential that you will both die. Or you will by protecting her." Fi added, walking behind Ms. Aumont a dark look hovered of her face.

Eric frowned at Fi.

"Whose side are you even on! I thought she was your friend too!" Eric cried.

"That's why she needs to leave. I don't want her to die Eric!" Fi snapped.

202

"She is with us we can protect her. Don't let mother get into your head!"

Eric shouted.

His back stiffened and his hands balled into fists, irritation surged inside

him.

His eyes darkened and warped into a miserable black, as if he had lost

all hope. The look of bitterness swept across his face.

Liv felt afraid, as if Eric had turned into a different person. He went to

lunge for his sister when he turned around and stormed off.

Suddenly, his mother grabbed his arm preventing him from leaving.

"We are not done." Ms. Aumont hissed.

"Let. Go. Of. Me. Now." His voice was so loud, so thunderous, that Eric

struggled to concentrate on what he was going to say next.

Liv backed up slowly, a cold, sharp chill of fear ran up her back as Eric

faced off with his mother and sister.

As she continued slowly backing away from the stand-off, a hard

unwelcoming pull came from her arm, Liv's eyes widened in fear as

before she could scream, a clammy hand covered her mouth.

High pitched ringing was going through Liv's ears, she tried to open her

eyes but was blinded by the whiteness of her surroundings. Everything

seemed like it was moving past, but Liv couldn't feel her legs moving.

She was being dragged. She struggled at the weights on her arms that

were pulling her forward but was too weak to fight it. Dipping in and out

of consciousness, she could hear people talking, one voice being

alarmingly familiar.

204

"You sure about this? How do you know this is the right girl?" An

unknown voice asked.

"I'm certain this is the one, look at her necklace! Her complexion! It's

Idun alright." Another replied.

Her eyes snapped open in terror as she squirmed and tried to fight them

off punching and kicking- no use. Kicked and punching them was like

hitting marble, impenetrable.

"Oh, look she's awake. Hello sweetheart, nice of you to join us." The

stranger holding her bicep laughed, squeezing her arm with such force

she winced as she could feel the bones creaking in her body.

"Let me go you shit!" Liv cried out in pain.

"Don't worry we are almost there then you'll be free."

Liv continued to struggle in response.

205

"If you don't come willingly, I will break your arm." The other stranger

snapped, putting more pressure on her arm.

Liv yelped. Is this it? Is this how she dies?

Hot tears stream down her cheeks like white hot metal and her head

flopped. In disbelief, she refused this to be her fate. Looking down she

realised she was wearing a white chiffon dress that was down to her

ankles. The smell of decaying flowers and incense burned her nostrils.

She looked up at the change of setting: the ceilings were high, and the

cold hard floors soothed the friction burns on her feet from being

dragged. Stained glass burst the white walls, pillars, and floor with

colour.

Pews were either side of the aisle filled with unknown figures as if this

was a ceremony of some sort. To Liv's realisation she was in some sort of chapel. In front of her was a stone alter. Liv struggled again as she

attempted to fight against her captors.

The closer she was escorted to her; Liv could see the stone alter had a

crest of some description engraved into it. To her horror it was the

Aumont family crest. A hooded figure had emerged from behind the

alter. Liv could just about make out a crooked smile from underneath it.

"Kneel." The hooded figure demanded.

Without thought, Liv complied with their demand.

Liv looked around, the people sat in the pews all wore black hooded

cloaks, the same as the one who commanded her to kneel. As Liv

thought, the voice had sounded very familiar to her, almost too familiar.

As she continued with the ritualistic practice, there was no sign of Eric.

Part of her was relieved to not see him or Fi in the pews. Part of her

dreaded that she was alone with no one to save her.

"Hands. Now." The hooded figure demanded.

Once again Liv complied as the Hooded figure yanked her hands forward

roughly and tied them up with scratchy old rope.

"Why are you doing this?" Liv whimpered.

The hooded figures smile turned twisted and unamused. They pushed

back their hood to reveal a familiar face.

It was Mr. Adler.

"You've deceived us for far too long Idun, it's time to pay up and give us

the immortality we deserve," Mr. Adler hissed.

To his right was a skinny taller hooded figure, who seemed to linger

behind a tall concrete pillar to the right of the alter.

208

"I'm not Idun. You've got the wrong idea." Liv exclaimed.

"No, he has not, you know extensive knowledge about Idun, and the apples that no normal person would know. You also wear that necklace that is also very similar to what the apples now look like." A female voice accused.

It was the lurking hooded figure, they had moved next to Mr. Adler, Liv knew exactly who this was before they lifted their hood. Ms. Aumont.

"Enough talk. Let's begin." Mr. Adler protested.

He approached behind Liv and tore the white linen dress she had on.

"Stand." He ordered.

Liv hesitated, frozen with fear that she was going to die.

"I said stand!" Mr. Adler hissed again and pulled Liv to her feet. He then cut off her underwear. Bare and vulnerable, Liv's untouched body was on display for all to see.

"Was there a need to strip the poor girl? You could have at least given her some dignity, Ajax!" Ms. Aumont exclaimed.

Liv started shaking, she could feel herself closing off every emotion- every sensation- she had, preparing herself for the end.

"You need to willingly lie down on the alter, please comply and this will all be over." Ms. Aumont whispered.

Liv nodded, confused with her tone, this was the nicest Ms. Aumont had spoken to Liv, almost with sincerity. Liv climbed onto the cold concrete alter. The crest engraved, dug into her back.

As she laid there while Mr. Adler was uttering a summoning of some

sort in Norse, Liv started feeling the anger bubbling within herself. How

could she be so pathetic? She had willingly complied with her captors

and allowed herself to be killed, like a lamb to the slaughter.

She wasn't helpless really. There must have to be something-anything! -

she could do to save herself. Burning with rage, she watched, Mr. Adler

hover a rusty archaic dagger over her belly button.

"Any last words Idun?" Mr. Adler sniggered.

"Go to Hell." Liv spat.

A sharp, stabbing hot pain began to overrun Liv's body.

Her body shuddered as the unbearable agony as the dagger contacted her

skin.

"Wait! Ajax, don't! Look-!"

Without any thought a bright burning light filled the room.

Was this it? Is this Heaven? Liv thought to herself.

Chapter Seventeen

A high-pitched ringing reverberated in Liv's ears. To her disbelief, she wasn't dead.

Her vision was fuzzy, but she could hear voices squabbling.

Shadowy figures were merging into each other in the pews violently.

The smell of smoke burned Liv's nose.

She winced as she turned her head to see where Mr Adler and Ms Aumont had disappeared. To her astonishment, her eyes found them as she scanned the room. Mr. Adler was crumpled on the floor as Ms.

Aumont was on top of him, wrestling the dagger out of his hand. Liv

tried to wriggle her hands, however the surge of pain ran through her

wrists. Water filled her eyes as the harsh smoke thickened in the room.

Liv closed her eyes wishing this was all just a bad dream.

To her surprise she felt cold clammy hands loosening the ropes on her

wrists and ankles.

"Stay still, Olivia," A stern feminine voice instructed.

A tall woman with ebony, unruly hair stood over her, her soft green eyes,

were unfamiliar to Liv. The woman hovered her hands over Liv's deeply

grazed stomach. Another bright light, not as bright as Liv witnessed

earlier, hummed over her navel. The gash that was there suddenly healed

into a fleshy coloured looking scar that sat above the surface of the skin.

"I'm so sorry, Olivia, I didn't even know what I was doing, your injury is healed as best as I can, but I couldn't heal it fully to leave you without a scratch." The woman quivered.

Liv looked up at the woman. To her realisation the woman, who seemed to have a personality transplant, was Ms. Aumont. She seemed younger, and much softer in her features.

Her chin and nose were smoothed and not as pointed, not a frown line could be seen on her face, but her charcoal hair wasn't entirely black, Liv noticed. It did have the odd streaks of silver that glistened in her hair.

"Ms. Aumont, are you feeling okay?" Liv asked in confusion.

Ms. Aumont looked up, over Liv's body and towards the stairwells. Liv followed her gaze and saw Fi standing at the top of the stairwells with a

215

fire extinguisher. She started pacing down the stairs energetically, a folded dressing down draped over her arm, waving the arm of the extinguisher around the edges of the bottom of the stairs.

She danced around the pews bashing people who came at her with her trusty extinguisher and sprayed the small flames that were around her.

Eventually she made it to a naked Liv and a shocked mother.

Fi threw her arm around Liv cradling her into a bear hug.

"Ohmigod, I'm so glad you're okay! Dad woke up and told us about what Ajax and Mother were up to." Fi explained, hanging the dressing gown around Liv's shoulders.

"Ophelia is that you?" Ms. Aumont choked.

Fi looked confused at her mother.

"What happened?" Fi snapped scowling at her.

216

"I can't remember, last time I saw you was when you were very small, look how much you've grown. Everything is blank after your uncle came to visit all those years ago when I first met your father. Then Olivia....

The light that came out of her was remarkable." Ms. Aumont explained.

"Heheee... t-t-truly remarkable..." a shaky voice spoke weakly.

It was Mr. Adler he was slumped sat against a pillar that Ms. Aumont was lurking behind previously. His eyes were wide and alert, his face was aged and ghastly. His voice trembled as he spoke not in fright, but with caution.

Fi attempted to lung at him, but Liv held her back.

"She's going to end us all..." He laughed hysterically.

His skin grew greyer, and his body was thin, the more Liv looked at him

the more she realised that he was ageing quickly, almost wisening in

front of their very eyes.

"What do you mean by that?" Ms. Aumont asked.

"You should have just complied. The curse that mother set on you for

marrying that man was working. Of course, the little girl had broken it."

Mr. Adler wheezed.

Fi narrowed her eyes at her decaying uncle.

"Leave him be, he's Hel's problem now," Fi hissed.

Mr. Adler laughed hysterically again. His feet started to disappear, then

his arms, then his torso until the black cloak he was wearing flopped on

the floor. A whirl of dust flew through the room and dispersed.

So many unanswered questions Liv had swimming through her head.

218

"where's Eric?" Liv asked Fi.

"He's with our father. But first you need to calm down Liv…" Fi

cautioned.

Looking down at her hands, Liv freaked, they were glowing as well as

her arms.

"Wha- what's happening to me?!" Liv exclaimed.

Ms. Aumont held Liv's hands in hers she looked at her calmly even

though her hands scalded hers. The sizzle of Ms. Aumont's hands

sounded like bacon beginning to fry, which made Liv queasy.

"Olivia, breathe." Ms. Aumont spoke calmly.

Liv breathed deeply then exhaled and repeated. The light died down and

the sound of sizzling flesh stopped. The stench of burning flesh made Liv nauseous. As she turned to the side that Fi and Ms. Aumont weren't on

and threw up.

"Good girl you're alright now." Fi soothed, smoothing Liv's messy

blonde hair.

"What am I?" Liv trembled.

"I believe that you might be a Deity, only a goddess with such power can

do what you did before you were almost sacrificed." Ms. Aumont

explained.

Liv looked at her in confusion - almost in denial over what she just

heard.

"We will need to take you to Asmund and see what he thinks he's always

been the more omniscient out of us all. Definitely a descendant of Odin."

Ms. Aumont chuckled.

220

"I don't think we need dad's confirmation, Mother. Have you had a look at what you look like recently?" Fi chipped in.

Ms. Aumont caught herself in the reflection of one of the shiny metal shields that had the family crest engraved that was hung on one of the walls. To her astonishment, she had realised that she had her youth restored to her.

"Oh my, she really is a Deity." Ms. Aumont gasped.

"I think we need a full family meeting, as well as to report on what happened to Ajax too." Fi explained maturely.

Liv was amazed how calm both Ms. Aumont and Fi was. She couldn't even comprehend how confused and scared she was in all of this. All she knew was that she longed to see Eric.

"Ms. Aumont, may I ask you something." Liv asked.

"Call me Lilith, and of course." Lilith replied.

"When you and Eric had that dispute, why didn't he come for me." Liv asked sadly.

"You need to realise it wasn't the real me that told him, but it was like looking through a mirror, I remember that I had told him that you had hit your head and were in critical condition in hospital, that your parents had you with them. I am so sorry Olivia. Truly." Lilith regrettably confessed.

"Take me to see him now. Please." Liv asked, gulping through the lump in her throat as she struggled to comprehend the sheer surrealism of what just transpired.

Chapter Eighteen

Lilith, Liv, and Fi gathered themselves up from the hard marble floor.

Liv winced slightly, even though her wound was healed, it still caused

her grief.

"Just take it slow Liv, you're most likely in shock." Fi warned,

supporting Liv's back.

The three of them left the now slightly singed room and started to make

their way up the blackened stairs.

"it's rude of me not to have asked, but how is your father, Fi?" Liv asked,

trying to make conversation to make the journey less awkward.

224

"He's doing well, it's a good job that we have fast healers in this family."

Fi jokingly replied.

as they made their way to the top of the stairs, Liv paused briefly to rest

her feet.

"Are you OK Olivia?" Lilith asked with concern.

This was the first time that Ms. Aumont had shown any real concern for

Liv's well-being. This made Liv feel slightly uncomfortable however,

pleased that this was the true Lilith Aumont that she was meeting.

"I'm fine, my ankles I just a little sore from being tied up with itchy old

rope." Liv replied.

Lilith smiled warmly gesturing her to walk ahead.

compared with the room they had just left, the hallways that led to the

bedrooms still seemed Immaculate.

225

There was not a single speck of dust to be seen on the soft red carpets that lined the hall. To Liv's right she walked past the familiar bedroom that was Fi's. she could just make out the Voile white curtains that hugged the posters of the bed from the crack that was left ajar when she had left.

The next room that she came across which, was a few doors down from Fi's room, was shut. There was a small poster in the top right of the door that stated, 'do not enter'. Liv chuckled to herself as she realised the mysterious room had belonged to Eric.

Ask the doors started to run out one was left in the corner before the hallway had split to go either left or right. Fi let go of Livs back and softly knocked on the door before entering. The door opened. Like the

226

Tardis out of Doctor Who, this room was definitely bigger on the inside.

The ceilings were tall, and alongside one of the walls was a grand

bookcase that looked like a small library.

Adjacent to the to this was small mahogany coffee table with two tall

armchairs that faced their backs to them, against the facing the chairs

was a lit fireplace. A fur rug was placed in the centre between the two

chairs and the coffee table. In one of the chairs sat Dr. Aumont. His hair

was matted from being laid down he was slouched in one of his chairs

with a book in his hand.

"Father, you should be resting." Fi sighed.

"Now who's the rebellious one hey Ophelia." Dr. Aumont laughed.

He had closed the book he was reading and balanced it on the arm of the

chair. He tucked away the circular reading spectacles into his pyjama top

pocket.

Liv looked at him carefully noticing that one of his kind brown eyes had

been covered by a black satin eye patch.

Dr. Aumont studied the three of us before his next sentence.

He looked at Liv concerned that she was in a worse state than a cracked

head this time. He then double backed on Lilith who smiled lovingly at

him.

The number of expressions danced on his face, first, it started off angry,

then softened, then became more confused.

228

"Who are you and what have you done with my wife." He exhaled in

relief.

"I'm the woman you fell in love with. It's quite the story that has

happened to me and I have Olivia to thank for it." Lilith began to

explain, looking at Liv smiling.

Dr. Aumont looked across at Liv and nodded gesturing her to take a seat

in the empty armchair. Liv approached the empty armchair across from

Dr. Aumont.

"So, dearest wife let's hear your side of things. Considering it was you

who did this to me." Dr. Aumont probed.

Lilith perched on the arm of Liv's chair pained at the tone of his voice. It sounded like he had scolded her but also was disappointed in her actions towards him.

"Well, I have recently learned from my late brother. That Mother put a curse on me. Guess she was disproving of our marriage. It's awful, I've grown up a horrible mother and a terrible wife. I feel like I have lost years of my life because of it. I won't blame it for what I did to you what I did to your eye, I am truly sorry, and I will plan to spend the rest of my life making it up to you and the children." Lilith started to explain then her voice cracked as she started to sob.

The room went silence for Dr. Aumont to process the first revelation that had been discovered.

"I'm sorry to hear that Ajax has passed. Can't say that he didn't have it coming Houses Odin and Hel have always had their differences." Dr. Aumont Consoled.

Even though Ajax Adler, was a terrible man for what he did he was still Lilith's brother that she had lost.

"What actually happened to him?" Fi asked.

Lilith and Liv both exchanged a look.

"The Goddess of Youth punished him for his greed for becoming immortal." Lilith replied informatively.

"Get out! Does that mean Liv is actually Idun!? Wow first dad actually like Odin now this!" Fi exclaimed excitedly.

"Calm down Ophelia. No Liv isn't Idun, but she is-"

231

"A Deity." Liv whispered.

"Yes, now Liv, can you tell me what happened. Assuming that they weren't successful in sacrificing you obviously." Dr. Aumont interrogated.

Liv stiffened in her chair trying to push back the memories of what had happened to her.

"The blade made contact with me, and I was slightly sliced open. However, a bright light blinded Ajax and Lilith and him were fighting over the blade. I thought I had died at first, but when I'm extremely anxious or angry this light has started appearing from my hands or arms it had scolded Lilith's hands." Liv explained.

Dr. Aumont 'hmm'd' and was deep in thought before replying to Liv. He

rubbed his eyepatch thinking on what to respond that wasn't going to

cause Liv any more trauma.

"May I see your necklace please Liv I will return it to you straight

away." He asked.

Liv took off the necklace that Eric had given her.

The small golden apple pendant glistened as it caught the fires light.

"It was a gift from Eric." Liv added.

She got up from her chair and placed it into Dr. Aumonts hand. He

examined it carefully and began to chuckle.

"Oh, the Gods and their silly tests they still put on their descendants!" Dr

Aumont laughed.

Lilith, Fi, and Liv looked confused at one another waiting for an explanation.

"This was in Erics possession to test him whether he wanted it for himself. The fact he returned it to you, a Deity of youth and possibly a direct descendant of Idun herself. Means that our house was blessed. Which is probably why you fell in love with each other and why you have a good relationship with Fi." Dr. Aumont explained.

"What about me though, why wasn't I punished and why was my curse broken dear?" Lilith asked.

"Well, as Liv explained, even when you were still cursed you went to stop Ajax, saving Idun's descendant from being sacrificed. This must

234

have pleased Idun and as a reward broke the curse placed on you. That's

one hell of a redemption I'd say!" Dr. Aumont finished explaining.

"Where's Eric now, I thought he was with you." Liv asked.

"I don't know, he wasn't with me, though he was very upset because of

what Lilith had told him." Dr. Aumont replied with concern.

He gave Lilith the "we will talk about that later" side eye before giving

the necklace back to Liv.

Liv put the necklace on fingering the golden apple pendent.

For a second Liv could hear the faintest of music. Liv looked at Fi, who

knew she could also hear it too and gave her a nod to go chase it.

"Thank you for your hospitality, Dr. Aumont. I must find Eric if you

don't mind." Liv thanked then apologised for her leave.

Dr. Aumont nodded as Liv paced out the room half jogging, half walking

to follow the trail of music.

"Liv! Liv wait a second!" Fi called after her.

Liv stopped and waited for Fi.

"You can't go seeing Eric naked! Dad also left a gift in my room for you

I'd open it before you go chasing tunes." Fi advised.

Liv looked down in embarrassment, completely forgetting that she was

naked under the dressing gown!

"Thanks Fi, I'll cover myself up, tell Asmund I said thanks again." Liv

replied.

She gave Fi a tight hug before making it towards her bedroom.

On the bed was a white box. Liv approached it and lifted the lid and the label that was addressed to her.

Inside the box was a beautiful pale blue skater dress as well as fresh underwear and some white strapped sandals.

Dr. Aumont was all about modesty after all.

She slipped on her fresh clothes and darted out of Fi's room once again to follow the music.

Chapter Nineteen

Music. A gentle, familiar tune echoed through the narrow hallways as

Liv made her way swiftly through the corridors of the house. She knew

exactly where the music was coming from this time.

Following the melody down the hall on a familiar path; the translucent

blue dress danced around her legs, chasing the beautiful song, it

continued to get louder, as if it was teasing her to find the source. The

music danced to her left, as she was greeted with the tight passageway once again. Her dress floated down to the knee without hesitation she opened the door to be greeted with Eric at the piano, playing Moonlight Sonata Movement 3. Erics head snapped up as he abruptly stopped playing. Gliding over a few wrong keys, he rushed towards Liv. At first, Liv thought she was about to be rugby tackled before being swooped up into Eric's tight embrace. His scent was intoxicating, he smelt like cinnamon burning on a log fire. Liv pulled him in closer, forcing herself to remember his scent, in a desperate vie to imprint it onto her. She looked up in awe at him; he looked shattered. His beautiful brown puppy dog eyes were slightly sunken in and surrounded by dark circles.

 His chin was hugged by a lovely five O'clock shadow that seemed out of character on his tanned face. Studying the beauty in front of her, she had noticed that he had furiously been playing with his hair, as always,

239

as it was a complete mess. Liv giggled as she tiptoed to try smooth it down. Eric closed his eyes and relaxed himself under her touch. The room was much lighter and less gothic than when she had first discovered it.

"You're really here, aren't you?" Eric whispered softly, nuzzling her neck.

Liv flung her arms around him and returned a tight embrace back.

"I'm here! I didn't have an accident, I have never left." Liv whispered back reassuringly.

Eric's bright white teeth flashed as he smiled, his face had seemed to have changed. From the lifeless look he had on while she had first entered the room. To the stunning relaxed and much more sentient look.

"What happened? All I know Is that my horrible mother was involved in this; I swear if she's- "

"Eric, calm down, there's a lot to explain so you had better sit down."

Liv interrupted quickly.

Eric looked at her, confused that she seemed to be defending his mother after the cruel way she had treated Liv.

The pair of them walked away from the concealed door and made their way to the black piano stool. They both rested themselves onto it as Eric looked at Liv waiting for the said explanation.

"Now please try keep an open mind. It's still very confusing to me." Liv started.

Erics eyes were focused on her intently. She knew she had his full attention.

241

"I know your secret, that you are a descendant of Odin. I also know that your uncle was a descendant of Hel, he tried to sacrifice me because he thought I was Idun's reincarnation. Unfortunately, he has passed away." Liv explained.

Erics eyes widened, and his eyebrows raised inquisitively.

"How did you find that out about us?" Eric laughed, impressed with Liv finding out so quickly.

"After I was almost sacrificed, Lilith saved me. She deterred your uncle away from me and disarmed him. She had changed or had awakened from a curse that your grandmother put on her for marrying into your house. We discovered this as it was your uncles' dying words to us." Liv continued.

At first Eric scoffed, in denial that his mother could have spared Liv. But the more he listened the more he started to believe her. Other than Fi and his father, Liv was the only person he truly trusted.

"So, you're telling me that Ajax was behind everything the whole time? Guess he had it coming. Though what about you? Are you alright." Eric trailed off, then questioned in worry.

"I'm fine, Lilith healed me. Got a battle scar to prove it, but I'll be okay. In fact, I'm _more_ than okay." Liv smiled.

Hesitating, as much as she wanted to tell Eric she was a Deity, she enjoyed the normality of their budding relationship. She couldn't tell him everything would change, and she couldn't live in his world full of Gods, Cultists and god knows who's what! She longed for a normal human life where they could both graduate and potentially start their lives together.

243

"I'm sorry this has happened to you… If you hadn't got involved with me this would never have happened." Eric sighed regretfully looking down.

"It wasn't your fault that I got hurt. You didn't know. I'm safe here and now, with you. And I can finally look at you and say this to you." Liv smiled, cupping his face in her hands. His stubble was rough against her hands, like a cat's tongue. Eric felt at ease when Liv reassured him.

"And what's that you want to say to me." He teased, leaning forward drawing closer to Liv's face.

She blushed furiously as she took every bit of self-control to refrain from kissing him yet.

"That… I… Love you." Liv stammered.

Eric grinned widely as he stole a kiss from her. His lips tasted like

spearmint as Liv returned the kiss, bringing him in closer craving more.

Eric pulled away chuckling.

"Easy tiger, you probably need some rest."

He took her hand into his and held it.

"Also, I've waiting a very long time to hear you say that to me. Because

I hope that you know that I have loved you from the moment, I met you."

Eric smiled.

Liv flushed once again, flattered by Erics returned feelings for her. She

had never had a boyfriend before. She was always waiting for the right

one to come along.

With his free hand Eric dabbled some of the piano keys in front of her.

The melodic tune indicated that the mood was happy and full of love.

Liv rested her head on his shoulder and slipped her hand out of his.

"Play me something beautiful." She asked.

Eric smiled at her.

"One beautiful song for one beautiful lady." He replied.

Kissing her forehead as he began to play "Pern" by Yann Tiersen. relaxed

her head on his shoulder closing her eyes, listening to him play the most

beautiful song she had ever heard. She was safe now.

<u>End.</u>

Printed in Great Britain
by Amazon

10471222R00144